The Corgi Chronicles

Laura Madsen

Alternate Universe Books
Salt Lake City, Utah
alternateuniversebooks.com

The Corgi Chronicles

ISBN: 978-1484842225

Printed in the U.S.A.
Cover art © by Sandara Tang.
Cover design © 2013 by Michelle Zumbrunnen.

This book is dedicated to my parents,
Ann and Neal McLain,
for giving me a love of reading and
writing, and to my daughters,
Bridget and Katelyn,
with the hope that they will love books
as much as I do.

Author's Note

My Pembroke Welsh Corgi was the inspiration for this story. Corgis are an ancient herding dog breed from Wales. As Pippin points out, the plural is technically *corgwyn*, or *corgŵn* in the Welsh spelling. There are two corgi breeds: the Pembroke Welsh Corgi has a stubby tail, while the Cardigan Welsh Corgi has a long tail.

As far as I know, corgis are not actually able to speak human languages or write books, but in Welsh mythology they do serve as steeds for fairies. Corgis are clever dogs, although they can be noisy barkers and they might try to herd you and your family members. For more information about corgis, see the Pembroke Welsh Corgi Club of America website at www.pembrokecorgi.org.

Chapter 1

I'm called Pippin. You wouldn't be able to pronounce my real name, a deep Welsh bark, but Pippin is what I'm called by my human family.

I'm a Corgi. Note the capitalization. Many humans neglect to use the capital *C*, but you really should.

We're an ancient race, distantly related to dogs. On the outside, we look similar to regular dogs, but our ears are bigger, our legs shorter, and our eyes more intelligent. Most humans have no clue that we're anything special. Even my human mom, Laura, who works as a veterinarian, thinks I'm a dog.

How we differ from dogs is our spark of magic. We are fairy stock. If you traced back the lineage of a regular dog five thousand years you would find wolves. Not so with us. If you traced back five thousand years you would find Kings of the ancient Corgwyn. (That's the Welsh plural of our name.)

Our kin are the fey: elves, fairies and sprites. We are the fairies' steeds—fairies are much too small to ride on horses, but we're a perfect size for riding. Many of us have a lighter stripe on our shoulders from our saddles rubbing. Mine is a tan stripe sprinkled through my black fur.

When I was born, eyes and ears closed like a common puppy's, I was already aware of my history and my task. Although Corgwyn are assigned to fairy masters or mistresses, many of us live with human families, passing as house dogs. This allows the fey to keep a closer eye on the activities of humans, the most numerous race on this planet.

My fairy mistress is named Aliiana. She's an earth fairy, based in the dry, rocky foothills to the south of my human home. She spends most of her time tending the granite base of the mountains, which in turn nurtures the plants and animals.

I speak with Aliiana nearly every day. Either she contacts me telepathically, or I sneak out when Laura isn't paying attention. I'm very fast and can easily run to the foothills and back before my human family notices I'm gone.

One day I received an urgent telepathic message from Aliiana.

Pippin! Her voice echoed in my mind. *You must come quickly!*

What's wrong, Mistress?

Just hurry, I'll explain when you get here.

I needed to get away from my human home as fast as possible, but my family was in the yard so I couldn't sneak out. I picked up a picture book in my mouth and carried it to the littlest girl. She smiled, took it from me, and held it up to Laura. "Read, please, Mom?" she asked in her tiny voice.

"Okay, sweetie," said Laura. She led the little girls back to the bedroom for story time.

As soon I was alone, I rushed out, slipped under the fence, and dashed away to the south. It was late winter, but the snow was compacted so I was able to trot on top of the crusted surface. Soon I arrived at Aliiana's home, a cozy burrow nestled under a stand of Gambel oaks. Her tunic was colored the grayish blue-green of sagebrush, and her pants were the dark olive green of junipers. She was hastily stuffing items into a pack.

"Pippin," she said, "we need to leave immediately. We've been summoned by the Prince of the Mountains."

"The Prince?" I asked. The Prince of the Mountains was an elf, among the most powerful of the fey. He had never contacted us before.

She nodded. "He must have an urgent reason to call us." Aliiana quickly buckled on my saddle and mounted. Her cloth pack was slung across her back, and her tiny longbow was strapped on the saddle. Even with all her equipment, it was still a light load for me to carry.

Corgwyn have a very accurate sense of direction and an instinctual notion of where to find a particular fey. I knew the Prince lived high in the Uintah Mountains, north and east of the city.

Getting out of the city was the hard part. Although Aliiana could make herself and her equipment invisible to humans, I was still visible, along with my saddle. I kept to the fields and alleys as much as possible.

At one point a girl with blonde curls saw me and ran toward us. "Hey, puppy!" she yelled. "Are you lost?

Come here, puppy." I ducked under a fence as I heard her call, "Mom! There's a puppy running loose!"

I made for a stand of trees bordering a city park, but before I reached it I saw the unmistakable shape of an Animal Control truck. *Uh-oh.* The blonde girl's mother must have seen me running full-bore down the street, and called Animal Control to have me picked up.

I ducked around behind a house, hoping to evade the officer, but the truck was waiting for me on the other side. The officer got out of the truck and approached me, slowly but menacingly. I looked over my shoulder—no escape route.

Mistress, I need help, I said telepathically.

Aliiana whispered in Elvish, quickly casting a spell. She released a white glowing ball from her hands that shot toward the officer's face. He blinked, then looked around in confusion.

Hurry, Aliiana said. *The confusion spell will only last a few minutes.*

I dashed around the dazed officer and made it to the trees.

Once we were safe in the foothills, I was able to run in a more direct route, dodging around junipers and oaks. Higher up the mountain, spruces and aspens dominated and we saw more wildlife. I wanted to stop to bark at a moose cow and calf that we spotted drinking from a stream, but I knew Aliiana was depending on me.

After many hours, we finally stopped to rest. I was tired, so Aliiana removed my saddle and lightly rubbed my sore muscles. She picked up each of my feet, inspecting my paw pads for injuries.

"I've got a surprise for you, Pippin." Aliiana winked, and pulled a dog treat from her bag. I know, I shouldn't have gotten so excited about a dog treat, but spending most of my life pretending to be a dog has affected me. The treat was quite yummy, by the way.

We both napped for a short time, Aliiana curled up against the soft fur of my neck. I was dreaming about chasing cats when she whispered, "Pippin, wake up. We must be on our way."

I ran several more hours, winding ever higher. The aspens were bare of leaves for the winter, and the blue spruces and ponderosa pines were laden with snow clumps. We finally arrived at a dense stand of lodgepole pines. The trees were tall and robust, and grew so close together that no snow reached the forest floor beneath.

Aliiana dismounted and led me under a low-hanging branch. Under the canopy of the pines, a large space opened up, warm and dry. The space was at least fifty yards across and ten feet high. Dry pine needles made a soft floor for my paws. The space was illuminated by glowing orbs hung from the branches: some yellow, some white, and some light green.

A number of elves sat in golden chairs scattered around the space. Some painted or read books, while others played harps or flutes. Most of the elves ignored us. A few of the younger ones nodded at Aliiana. Only one spoke to us.

"Greetings, fairy. Greetings, *elranor*." (That's the Elvish word for us furry fairy steeds.) The speaker was a male elf with braided blond hair and twinkling green eyes.

"Greetings, sir elf. I'm Aliiana, and my Corgi is called Pippin. We have been summoned by the Prince."

"We've been expecting you," he said. "My name is Nelathen. Come; I'll take you to the Prince."

We followed Nelathen deeper into the pine dwelling. In the center of the pines, the Prince sat on a gilded chair set on a raised platform. When he saw us, he put aside the blue leather-bound book he had been reading and stood. He was very tall and thin, with glittering blue eyes and golden hair. Like all fey, his ears were pointed.

"Aliiana, thank you for coming so quickly." He looked at me and winked. "Your steed must be very fleet of foot." Turning back to Aliiana, he added, "A great danger has come to the fey, and we need your help. Let's discuss matters over supper."

We followed the Prince to a small grouping of chairs nearby. Aliiana is only two feet tall, while the Prince stood as tall as a human. He gently lifted her onto a velvet chair and then sat on a carpet on the ground so that they could speak face-to-face. The other elves brought water and elven bread for Aliiana and the Prince, and meat for me.

After a few minutes, the Prince set down his goblet and folded his elegant hands. "The Ruseol Gem has been stolen."

Aliiana gasped. I just cocked my head to the side—I had never heard of the Ruseol Gem.

The Prince saw my confusion and explained. "The Ruseol Gem is as old as the universe and is the source of all good magic on this planet. The elves, dwarves, fairies and sprites all channel its magic in different ways, but ultimately their magic comes from the Gem. The elves and dwarves have protected it from time immemorial." He took another sip of water, and leaned forward. "I have just received word from the Queen, who in turn received word from King Latrak of the dwarves. Someone, or something, stole the Gem from its hiding place. It was buried deep within a solid piece of granite thirty feet across. I've asked for your help, Aliiana, because of your specialty with granite."

"What does the Gem look like, sir?" I asked.

"An excellent question, *elranor*. I have never set eyes upon it, but the tales say it is a reddish-purple, more beautiful than the finest diamond, and larger even than you."

"And what is known of its theft?" Aliiana asked.

He sighed. "We're very concerned. No one knew its location except the royalty of the elves and dwarves. I fear the being who is powerful enough to have removed it from the granite." His eyes were distant as he sat back. "If the Gem were to be destroyed, it would mean the end of good magic—and the end of the magical races, from dwarves and elves to goblins and dryads."

"But, sir, how are we to find it, just a fairy and a Corgi?" I asked.

The Prince smiled and patted the top of my head. "You won't be alone on this quest, my young Corgi friend. Nelathen will accompany you, as well as two others."

"Where should we start our search?" Aliiana asked.

"I suggest starting at the place where it was kept for millennia. The Gem was hidden deep within the mountains north of here, in the place called Montana by the humans. There is a group of dwarves who guard the site. They may be able to give you more details about the theft." He smiled gently. "In the meantime, I suggest you rest. My folk will pack supplies for your trip."

"Sir," I said hesitantly. "How long might we expect to be away on this quest?"

"Weeks, at least, I should expect. Possibly months."

My big ears drooped. I was afraid that my human family would worry that I had run away or been harmed. Although I can speak the human language, I couldn't contact them without blowing my cover.

Aliiana understood the cause of my sadness. "It will be all right, Pippin." She hugged me around my neck. "I'm sure your human family will be fine. They'll be happy to see you when we return."

Nelathen showed us to a quiet corner of the pine dwelling where we could rest. I circled around several times before settling on a green silk cushion. Aliiana snuggled against my fur to keep warm, and we both slept. When we woke, I could tell from the quality of light filtering through the pine boughs that it had snowed again.

Aliiana stretched and patted my head. "Are you ready to start our adventure, Pippin?"

"I'm a bit nervous," I said. "I'm not sure how we'll find the Gem."

She tickled my big ears. "We will have help, and we will be strong. You and I make a good team."

The Prince appeared suddenly, moving on silent feet. "Aliiana, Pippin. Are you ready to meet the others?"

The Prince led us toward the entrance of the pine dwelling. Nelathen was bent over, stuffing equipment into a large leather pack. A sprite flitted around his head. Sprites are the smallest of the fey, as small as a robin or blue jay. They also have wings, unlike the elves and fairies.

"You've already met Nelathen, of course, and this is Birgitte." The Prince gestured to the sprite, who stopped fluttering and landed gracefully on the pack. She was tiny, with pale green skin, hair and wings, and darker green clothing.

"It's very nice to meet you, Birgitte," said Aliiana.

"Thank you," Birgitte replied in a voice so high-pitched that only a fey or Corgi could hear.

"Birgitte has extraordinary magical abilities for her kind," the Prince explained. "Her magic, combined with her ability to remain undetected from many eyes, will make her an asset to you on your quest."

"And you mentioned another member of this party?" Aliiana asked.

Nelathen straightened, smiled, and whistled. An enormous cat approached from the shadows of the pine trunks.

I will admit I was frightened.

My hackles rose, my ears pinned back and I growled. The cat glared at me with piercing amber eyes. Aliiana placed a hand on my back and whispered into my ear, "Manners, Pippin."

I stopped growling (mostly) but kept my hackles up. One of my favorite hobbies at my human home is to wrestle with my cat housemate. I outweigh him by double, and use my size to my advantage, tackling him down to slobber on his neck. But this cat outweighed me by at least triple, and didn't look friendly.

I recognized him as a mountain lion, or cougar, from a television show that my human family had watched on *Animal Planet*. I knew that cougars lived throughout our state, and could be ruthless hunters. What was this monster doing in our company?

"Aliiana, Pippin, this is Barrol," said Nelathen. "He is my familiar—my magical animal companion."

Aliiana took a step toward the beast, extending her hand for him to sniff. I growled again. The cat seemed to smirk at me.

"Don't worry, little brother," he rumbled. "I won't eat your fairy." He sat down on his haunches and added, seemingly as an afterthought, "I probably won't eat you, either."

Uh-oh, I thought. *I'd better watch my furry little bottom.*

Chapter 2

Nelathen finished packing the large leather bag and strapped it onto his back with a quiver of arrows. "I've made some packs for you and Barrol as well," he said to me, "to help carry more food."

He produced two sets of saddle bags, and fitted the larger around Barrol's chest and the smaller around mine. Aliiana's saddle fit comfortably on my back between the bags. I turned my head, catching the appealing scent of meat jerky from my bags. Nelathen saw my movement and laughed. "That's for later, *elranor*. We need to watch our rations."

Nelathen finally strapped a sword belt around his waist and took up his longbow, which was unstrung to use as a walking staff. Aliiana strapped on her own little pack and bow and hopped lightly into my saddle. The sprite seemed to have no equipment except for a tiny bag tied to her waist. It was so small it would barely hold a single dog treat.

We all walked together to the entrance of the pine dwelling. The Prince stood just outside, lightly balancing on the top of the new-fallen snow. A shaft of sunlight pierced the forest to sparkle on his golden hair. Many of the other elves from the community stood around him with hopeful expressions.

Nelathen and Aliiana bowed to the Prince. It's hard to bow when you walk on four legs, but the monstrous cat and I both dipped our heads in respect.

"My friends," the Prince began, "I have asked the five of you to set out on this quest because I feel you are our best hope. Aliiana, you have empathy for granite and can discover how the Ruseol was stolen. Nelathen, you have knowledge of the world and can guide Aliiana. Birgitte, you have powerful magic abilities and can help Aliiana recover the Gem. And Pippin and Barrol, you are both loyal and can protect her. I give you all my blessings for a rapid, safe and successful conclusion to your quest. I also give you each a gift to speed you on your way."

The Prince held up five necklaces of finest silver chain, each with a dangling emerald pendant that glittered green in the sunlight. Although the jewels were identical in style, they ranged in size from miniscule for the sprite to enormous for the cougar.

When the Prince fastened my necklace around my furry neck (along with the collar I wore from my human home, with its identification and rabies tags), he whispered, "Farewell, *elranor*."

The snow started up again soon after our departure. I had trouble plowing through with my short legs, and after a while I decided to let Nelathen and his cougar blaze the trail. I followed behind in their footsteps, which made for easier going.

Birgitte, the sprite, flew for the first few hours, but a fierce cross-wind began to gust. We were afraid she would be blown right into a tree trunk. Nelathen offered to carry her, and tucked her tiny body into the hood of his cloak. She sat on his shoulder, peeking out.

"Are you keeping up, little brother?" the cougar asked.

I felt fatigue in my legs but certainly wasn't going to admit that to an overgrown kitty. "I'm fine," I replied. "I could keep running for hours. That's why the fairies chose us Corgwyn, you know. We're nimble, fast and strong."

The cougar made a laughing sort of rumble in his throat. After he turned back to the trail, I bared my teeth at him. Aliiana lightly swatted my rump to remind me of my job.

Crack!

A loud percussion sounded, echoing off the valley walls, and was followed by a high-pitched *whizzz* overhead.

"Get down!" yelled Nelathen.

Aliiana leapt off my saddle and we took cover behind a snow bank. Nelathen and the cougar shared a glance, exchanging silent words, and nodded. Nelathen's form wavered, turning translucent lavender before completely disappearing. Although he was invisible, I could tell by his slight footprints in the snow that he dashed off to the north. Barrol took off to the south, bounding through the snow while keeping to the shadows.

"What do you think that was?" I whispered to Aliiana.

"Gunshot," she replied. "Where's Birgitte?" she asked, looking around.

"Over here," came a whispered reply from a small shrub.

Crack!

There was another shot, and a huge pile of snow slumped down from a tree, landing right behind us.

I couldn't see Nelathen or his cougar and I was worried for their safety—and ours.

Then I heard a human male voice swearing. "Missed him again," the voice grumbled.

Soon another voice said, "Oof! Who do you think you are?" and was silenced.

Nelathen's voice called out. "All clear! Birgitte, I think we have need of your skills."

Birgitte emerged from the shrub and flew off, her tiny wings whirring. Aliiana hopped back on my saddle and I ran to follow.

We found Nelathen and the cat in a small clearing. Two human men lay face-down in the snow, quietly moaning. They both wore insulated camouflage jackets, pants, and boots. Their rifles stuck out of a snow bank twenty feet away. Nelathen stood over the men with his unstrung bow, which he had used as a staff to knock them on their heads. Barrol stood on the other side of the humans, rumbling deep in his throat and baring his huge fangs.

"Poachers," the cougar growled. "They were shooting at me. Fortunately, their marksmanship was amateur."

I gasped. "They were shooting at you?" Even though I was intimidated by the cat, I couldn't imagine humans trying to harm him.

"Indeed, little brother. But the season closed a month ago in this area, so they were trying to poach illegally."

"How do you know about hunting seasons?"

He smiled his big furry lips. "Think about it, little brother. If there were a Corgi-hunting season, wouldn't you pay attention to it?"

I nodded, my big ears drooping. One of the hunters stirred, starting to revive.

"Quickly, Birgitte," called Nelathen, waving her over.

Birgitte fluttered to the hunters and dipped a tiny hand into the bag at her waist. She pulled out a handful of a sparkling yellow powder and sprinkled it on the men's heads. She muttered a few Elvish words in her high-pitched voice, and then turned to the rest of us. "Let's go," she said, "and don't forget to cover our tracks. When they wake up, they won't remember any of this, and they'll find the idea of hunting to be repulsive."

Nelathen chuckled as he and Aliiana brushed out our tracks with pine branches.

We were a few miles past the hunters when the sky started darkening. "We'd better find a place to set up camp," Aliiana said to Nelathen.

"Aye," he said. "Barrol, would you scout a spot?"

The cougar bounded up the slope and disappeared into the underbrush. He reappeared a few minutes later and growled, "Follow me."

I scurried up the slope after him, anxious to settle into our camp. He had found a dry nook that was protected by a large boulder and several pines. The fey began to set up camp. Nelathen spread a weather-proof elven blanket from the boulder to the tree trunks to give us shelter.

Aliiana rummaged in the packs, retrieving a pan and some food. She quickly laid a fire of dry twigs, with pine needles as kindling. Within a few minutes, the fire roared and crackled. Aliiana melted snow in the pan and added some delightful elven ingredients to make a hearty stew. I lapped at the delicious stew, and also munched on some meat jerky. Feeling satisfied, I curled up near the fire with my nose tucked under my forepaws and fell asleep.

The storm passed over during the night, leaving a fresh, sparkling blanket of snow the next morning. The sky was crisp blue with just a few high clouds. The sun glistened on the snowy bare branches of the aspens. We quickly broke camp. I did my part by vigorously digging snow onto the embers of the fire, which hissed and steamed as they were extinguished.

Nelathen and Aliiana checked the map. Although we Corgwyn have an excellent sense of direction, we have difficulty interpreting maps. After the fey had decided on our route of travel, Aliiana summarized it for me.

"The Gem's resting spot is in the high mountains near a glacier which the humans call Sperry Glacier. It's in the humans' Glacier National Park." She gestured to the mountains. "We need to continue northwards for several more days. When we get to areas with sparser human populations, we'll be able to travel through the foothills instead of the high mountains. We'll need to cross a few wide interstate highways, which we'll try to time for early morning when the humans aren't around." She tickled my ears. "Are you going to be able to keep running, Pippin?"

I stood as tall as I could on my short legs. "I will carry you all the way, Mistress."

"Good," she said, and bent to kiss my wet nose. "I think you're the noblest steed any fairy has ever ridden."

The next few days passed uneventfully. The weather cleared, although temperatures grew colder as we went farther north. When we needed to cross the human highways, we tried to locate the occasional paths cut under the highway which are meant to allow wildlife to cross safely. The paths were designed for moose and mule deer, but worked just fine for our odd group.

Late one day, we passed near a small town in northern Montana, close to the national park.

"Let's camp here for tonight," Nelathen said. "I'll go into town to restock some of our supplies. I can also ask the humans about any unusual events in the park."

Nelathen pulled a bright red hat from his pack. It bore a logo for a human snowboard manufacturer. He put it on, pulling it down to cover his pointed ears. He unstrapped his sword belt, quiver, and pack and laid them in a sheltered area in the trees. Taking a deep breath, he tucked his shoulders forward and loosened his posture. In an instant he was transformed from an ageless, elegant elf to a slouching human snowboarder.

"Humans see only what they expect to see," he said. "Come on, Pippin. You can pretend to be my dog."

I barked in excitement as Aliiana removed my saddle. I trotted along beside Nelathen as we approached a convenience store on the outskirts of town.

"Remember not to talk," he said as we entered the store through automatic sliding glass doors. I woofed obediently.

"Hey," a poorly-groomed human teenager said from the counter.

"Heyyy," Nelathen drawled, perfectly imitating a Utah human accent. Nelathen wandered around the store, grabbing several bags of organic trail mix, some fresh fruit, and a loaf of whole-grain, organic cranberry bread. "Not as good as elven bread, but it's passable," he said in a low voice. He also picked up a bag of Uncle Rover's Super Yummy Bacon Strips for Dogs. "You deserve a treat," he said, smiling down at me. I wagged my little nubbin of a tail enthusiastically.

Nelathen laid our purchases on the counter, and added a Montana road map.

"Cool dog," the teenager behind the counter remarked as he scanned the items. I remembered that I was supposed to be posing as a regular dog, but I couldn't help but bark at the compliment.

"We're on our way to the park," Nelathen said. "Anything we should know about?"

The scruffy teenager shrugged. "Snow pack's good for boarding. They said it sounded like someone was dynamiting east of Lake McDonald Lodge last week, but they couldn't find anyone. Maybe seismic activity, they said."

"Hmm." Nelathen paid for our items with human cash. "Thanks."

"Okay, dude. Have fun."

When we returned to the campsite, Aliiana was fixing supper and Barrol was gathering large branches for the fire. Birgitte fluttered near Aliiana, babbling excitedly in Elvish.

Aliiana smiled at me. "Did you have fun, Pippin?"

"The clerk liked me!" I wagged my stubby tail. "Oh, and we heard some interesting news."

Nelathen nodded. "The clerk said there were reports of loud sounds in the area of Sperry Glacier. Authorities weren't able to determine the source of the disturbance."

Aliiana frowned. "What do you think it might have been?"

"Before we left the Prince, he and I spoke about what creature could possibly have removed the Gem. I'm not sure even a troll could manage that task; whatever creature is involved might be quite large and noisy."

Large and noisy and worse than a troll, I thought. *That sounds like something that might eat a Corgi.*

Nelathen saw my worried expression, tore open the bag of dog treats and tossed me a bacon strip.

Mmmm... I gobbled down the first, and he threw me another. Remembering my manners, I politely asked the cougar, "Would you like a bacon strip?"

Barrol wrinkled his snout. "No, thank you, little brother. I'll catch some hares later tonight."

After we ate a meal of meat jerky, fruit and organic whole-grain bread, the fey continued the discussion of the Gem. Now that we were getting close to Sperry Glacier, the next part of our mission loomed uneasily in our minds.

"Do you expect trouble from the humans when we enter the park?" Birgitte asked.

"I don't think so," Nelathen said. "It's a large area of land, very rugged. There are humans at the entry stations, so we'll have to enter overland. We should be able to maneuver up the mountains to the glacier without being seen."

"And where will we find the dwarves?"

"They have a series of tunnels dug into the mountain above the glacier. The Prince gave me written instructions from King Latrak to locate the entrance."

Aliiana looked troubled. "Did the Prince say whether any of the dwarves were injured during the theft?"

"The King's message was brief, but my impression is that the dwarves were unaware of the theft until after the fact."

"Despite the noise the clerk reported?"

Nelathen shrugged. "I hope we'll be able to learn more when we meet the dwarves."

Chapter 3

The next morning we started early. The sun was barely peeking over the eastern mountains as we approached the park boundary. Coming from the south, we had to slip across the human road and scale the park fence. Birgitte fluttered over the fence, Aliiana nimbly climbed, and Barrol clawed his way up a pine tree to jump down on the other side. Nelathen had to lift me over, though.

We were still about forty miles from Sperry Glacier. We made our way along ridges and saddlebacks, and passed several other glaciers.

Barrol usually ranged out ahead of us, scouting the path. At one point, he suddenly bounded back to us, growling a warning. A pair of human heads popped up over a ridge.

"Hey!" yelled one of the humans. "Look out!"

Barrol and I ducked out of sight, and the smaller fey made themselves invisible. Nelathen quickly tossed his sword and bow behind a boulder and pulled his hood forward to cover his pointed ears. I peeked out as he approached the humans.

"What's wrong?" he asked.

"Cougar," said one, a tall man in a bright yellow coat. "We saw a cougar run up this way. You need to be careful if you're hiking alone."

"Hmm, thanks. I didn't see one, but I'll be careful."

"Okay, well, have a good day."

"Yeah, you too."

After the humans were out of sight we regrouped. Nelathen pulled out the map. "There's Gunsight Lake, and that's Gunsight Mountain, so we need to climb up that ridge. Sperry Glacier is just on the other side of the ridge."

We crested the sharp, bare rocks at the top of the ridge. There were patches of snow caught in the crevasses, and the wind whipped furiously around us. The cold made my eyes burn and my nostrils freeze. Nelathen pointed down at the glacier. From above, it looked like a massive mound of snow slowly leaking down the valley. Below the glacier were several frozen lakes, glistening pale blue.

Nelathen pulled out the parchment of instructions from the dwarven king. He chuckled to himself and said, "Too bad the dwarves refuse to use human technology. A GPS would make this easier." He handed the parchment to Aliiana.

"'From the third rise sunward of the father peak,'" she read, "'stride earthward for one thousand, seven hundred and thirty-four paces, turn moonward and stride for eight hundred sixty paces, then delve beneath the skystone.'" She looked at Birgitte. "I think a 'skystone' is a meteorite, but do you understand the rest of the directions?"

Birgitte buzzed her wings and nodded. "I believe from my studies of dwarven culture that 'sunward' is east, 'moonward' is west, and 'earthward' would mean to descend the mountain."

It wasn't hard to find the third rise east, but once we started down the slope, we realized that we didn't know the dimensions of a dwarf's pace. Dwarves are shorter than elves, but taller than fairies, so a pace would probably be somewhere between their strides. We scrambled down the mountain a fair distance, clambering over boulders and at times slipping on icy pebbles.

Nelathen stopped, held his hand to shield his eyes from the glare of the sun, and looked around. "It could be anywhere, and I don't see any rocks that look like iron ore." His voice was strained from frustration.

Aliiana leaned forward in her saddle and said to me, "You've got a strong nose, Pippin. Do you think you might be able to sniff our path for us?"

I looked back and saw her encouraging smile. "I can try," I said.

Aliiana climbed off my back and quickly removed my saddle. "So you can move easily," she explained. I gave her a quick lick on her cheek and set my nose to the ground.

Sniff sniff sniff... I smelled the two human men we had passed earlier. *Sniff sniff sniff...* Then something big, maybe a bear, and little rodents hiding in the rubble. I moved away from the group to concentrate. Thirty yards away, I smelled another scent. At first I thought it was Barrol's, but I realized this scent was different—earthy and damp. I followed the scent further down the mountain and to the west, and it grew stronger. I was on the trail! I turned around and barked at the others, then waited while they scrambled down to me.

"Did you find something?" Aliiana asked.

"Yes, Mistress, a scent I don't recognize." I put my nose to the ground again and followed the trail a few more minutes.

Suddenly, I came across another scent—strong, bitter and hairy. I was so startled that I barked aloud. It reminded me of an opossum I had chased once, but much stronger. The two scents seemed to converge at a smooth, dark red boulder.

"The meteorite!" said Aliiana. "Good boy, Pippin." She rubbed my ears and kissed the top of my head.

"Good job, *elranor*," said Nelathen. "Now we 'delve,' as the dwarves say." He put his hands on the meteorite and slowly circled around it. Aliiana bent low and put her hands on the granite underneath our feet. Both were quiet. I sat down to rest my paws.

After a few minutes, Nelathen spoke. "I can't figure out how to get under it."

Aliiana shook her head. "The granite hasn't been disturbed from digging, so we must be meant to move the meteorite."

Nelathen looked at the meteorite, then at our meager party. "Dwarves have considerable strength." He nodded to Barrol, and then hunched low to put his shoulder against the meteorite. Barrol also leaned against the iron boulder, digging his huge claws into the rubble. They both groaned with the effort, but the meteorite didn't budge.

I hurried over and tried to push as well, bracing my paws against a rock. Above, I saw Birgitte flutter over, sprinkling her golden dust on the three of us. All of a sudden, I felt as strong as a mastiff. We all pushed one more time, and the meteorite rolled to the side.

"I did it!" I barked, and the others laughed.

Aliiana knelt by the hole which had been revealed. She placed her hands on the rim and concentrated. "This tunnel extends straight into the mountain, and seems to be dwarven-crafted."

I sniffed the air. "Both scents are getting stronger."

"Let's go," said Nelathen.

We had no need of light as we entered the tunnel, as all of us—a Corgi, a predator, and three fey—had excellent night vision. Aliiana and I took the lead because Nelathen and Barrol had to duck their heads under the low ceiling. Aliiana walked beside me as I sniffed along. Both scents were getting much stronger—the earthy smell that I thought was probably the dwarves, and the foul opossumish scent.

The tunnel eventually widened out into a chamber. Aliiana whispered to Nelathen. "Are we supposed to announce our presence?"

"I was expecting some sort of guard," he whispered. "King Latrak's instructions say to 'hammer thrice and thrice again, hammer on the delving meet.'" He turned to Birgitte. "Do you know what that means?"

"The delving meet should be some sort of pedestal," she said, "where dwarves would gather. You need to hammer on it to make a noise."

"Barrol, Pippin. See if you can find a pedestal."

The cougar and I crisscrossed the chamber quickly. Near the far wall we found a smooth stone column rising from the floor. I barked for the others, and stood up on my hind paws for a closer look. On the top of the column was a smooth bowl-like depression, with silver runes inlayed around the edges.

After joining us, Nelathen walked around the bowl, peering at the runes. "There are Elvish and Dwarvish runes here. The Elvish tell of great danger." He drew his long sword and held it upright to strike the pommel into the bowl.

Boom boom boom... Boom boom boom...

The sound was much louder than it should have been for metal against stone. It seemed to echo not only through the chamber, but into the ground beneath us.

Nothing happened for a few minutes. Then I felt rough hands grasp my head and neck.

Chapter 4

The dwarf who held me was as immovable as a rock. I squirmed and wriggled, and I might have tried to bite him, but his arms around my neck and chest were solid. And stinky. The earthy scent had definitely been dwarven in origin.

"Peace!" yelled Nelathen. "We're here on behalf of King Latrak!"

"Do you have proof of that?" the leader of the dwarves asked.

"Here." A dwarf held Nelathen's arms, but he somehow managed to free a hand to produce the parchment. "Your king's seal is on this document, as is the seal of my Queen Elspeth."

The dwarf leader snatched the parchment. He muttered some words and the seal glowed purple. "It's authentic," he said. The iron arms released me, and I spun around to growl at my attacker.

Six dwarves stood in a circle around us. It looked like it had taken three of them to restrain Barrol, and he was still snarling after being released. The dwarves were all thickly built, with shaggy beards and leather armor.

"My apologies," said the leader. "We can't be too careful these days. I'm Gornak. This is my brother Jurtug, and the others are members of my clan."

Nelathen introduced us, and Aliiana stepped forward. "I've been sent here to investigate the theft," she said. "I need to know everything that happened, and I need to see the place where the Gem was kept."

Gornak nodded. "Of course. But may we offer you some refreshment and rest before we get to business?"

My stomach grumbled at the word 'refreshment,' and I barked. The others agreed, and Gornak gestured for us to follow him. He approached a section of the chamber wall, roughhewn like every other section. His thick fingers delicately tapped a series of faint protrusions, and the section slid away. I like to think I'm a pretty observant Corgi, but I never would have detected the hidden door.

We followed the dwarves down another passageway, this one smooth and lit by gas lamps. They led us to a large chamber with vaulted ceilings and decorative stone and metal carvings. In the center of the room an enormous table of flawless cream-colored marble was surrounded by stone chairs and benches.

"Sit, please." Gornak gestured. I hesitated—when I'm pretending to be a dog, I'm not allowed on furniture. "You, too," he added, nodding to Barrol and me. I smiled my furry lips and hopped up onto a bench.

I was drooling by the time the dwarves brought us the meal. They brought bread and fruit for the fey, and meat for themselves. The platter they set before me held a magnificent piece of rare elk meat. I ate every bit of it, and licked the platter clean. I had decided that dwarven food was much tastier than elven food.

As I licked my lips a final time, I thought to pay attention to the conversation.

"—intruders?" Aliiana was asking.

"No, we were completely unaware," Gornak said. "The six of us work shifts of eight hours, with two dwarves on each shift. We take our work very seriously. The granite which housed the Gem was never unattended."

"Then how could it have been stolen?"

Gornak's red eyebrows and shaggy beard drooped. "I don't know."

One of the other dwarves spoke. "I was on duty when it happened. I saw nothing. We were performing our routine patrols, and I was on the far side. When I returned to the near side, I saw the hole in the rock. No one was there."

"Was there anything else of note?" Aliiana asked. "A smell? A sound?"

The dwarf chewed on his elk steak as he thought. "There was something," he said. "I didn't think of it until now, but when I was on the far side of the patrol, I heard a sort of high-pitched buzzing." He shrugged. "That's all. I'm sorry."

"And who was the other dwarf on duty?" Aliiana asked.

"I was," said Jurtug. "I was on the near side while he was on the far side. But I don't remember. I was walking patrol, felt a little dizzy, and then... it was over."

"Could be a confusion spell," Nelathen said. "That would explain the buzzing sound and your dizziness."

The fey and the dwarves talked for a bit longer, but I felt sleepy with my full tummy, so I curled up on the stone bench and took a little nap. Later, I was vaguely aware of strong arms gently lifting me and placing me on a soft cushion.

I slept for hours. I guess the long trek from Utah to Montana had tired me out more than I wanted to admit. When I awoke, I found myself in a cozy side chamber furnished with layers of wool rugs and soft pillows. I stretched and padded out to find everyone else.

The dwarves and fey were still in the main chamber. Aliiana was deep in discussion with Gornak but looked up at my approach. "Hello, Pippin. I'm glad you're awake. Gornak is about to show us to the site where the Gem was kept."

We followed the dwarves along a series of tunnels that grew rougher and colder as we went down. Finally, we arrived at the site. There really wasn't anything remarkable about that particular chunk of granite to set it apart from any other in the mountain. The tunnel simply ended at a large flat rock face, and a smaller tunnel looped around behind.

In the center was a gaping hole. Above the hole an ominous message was scrawled in red: *Angarath was here! The power will be mine!*

"Who's Angarath?" I asked.

"We don't know," said Gornak. "Do you?" he asked the fey.

The others shook their heads. "It means nothing to me," said Aliiana.

"The message suggests that this Angarath stole the Gem to take its power," said Birgitte.

"But how could its power be taken?" asked one of the dwarves.

Birgitte just shrugged and shook her head.

I approached the hole for a closer look. Parts of the hole were smooth, as if the rock had melted, while other parts were covered by deep angry scratches. The scent I had picked up earlier of monster-opossum was particularly strong.

Nelathen ran his fingers along the scratches. "Troll." He turned to me. "That may help us, because you can track the troll's scent."

Gornak gestured to the melted rock. "The dwarves have no magical capabilities to melt granite."

Nelathen shook his head. "Nor do the elves." He turned to Birgitte with a questioning look on his face.

She fluttered over and laid a dainty green hand on the melted stone. She shrieked and jerked her hand back as if burned, but I couldn't feel any heat. "This is dark, dark magic. I've never encountered anything like it."

"Do trolls have magic?" I asked.

"No, *elranor*," Nelathen said. "They're monstrous brutes but non-magical. And a troll wouldn't be clever enough to even find this place, let alone evade the dwarves' detection."

"I fear an evil wizard is behind this crime," said Birgitte. Nelathen nodded sadly.

Aliiana took a deep breath and approached the granite. She put her hands on the rock at the edge of the wall and very slowly made her way closer to the yawning hole. Through our telepathic link, I felt her becoming more agitated. I went to her, and poked my cold nose against her arm. She put one hand on my back to steady herself, and continued pressing toward the hole with her other hand.

Her breath came in ragged bursts and sweat drenched her face by the time she reached the hole. She let go and turned to speak. "The granite is in pain—it's burning. I've never felt such a thing, even when there have been wildfires in the foothills at home." She rubbed her eyes and continued. "The stone is in such pain that I can't get a clear picture of what happened, but it does confirm that there was dark magic done." She looked at Nelathen and Gornak. "Elven and dwarven magics were also done."

"Impossible!" said Gornak, waving his arms in anger. "No dwarf would ever take the Ruseol. And no dwarf would ever cause pain to the living rock of this mountain."

Nelathen laid a gentle hand on Gornak's shoulder. "We're not accusing you of anything. I agree that no dwarf would have done this, and I can assure you that no elf would have, either." Turning to the rest of us, he said, "I fear that this Angarath may have placed an elf and dwarf under his control, as well as the troll."

Gornak settled down and his face returned from red to tan. "Aliiana, is there anything we can do to relieve the granite's pain?"

"I'm not sure," she said. She turned to Birgitte. "Perhaps a healing spell?"

Birgitte nodded. "I will need help to enter the hole. Pippin, would you assist me?"

I barked, happy to help. She flew to me and settled on the back of my neck, holding on to my fur and peeking between my big ears. She was so light that I could barely feel her weight.

The hole was several feet above the floor level. I couldn't quite jump high enough, so Nelathen lifted me. As he set me down I winced, expecting my paws to burn, but the melted rock was cool and smooth beneath my toes. Birgitte huddled deeper into my fur as I walked slowly forward. The hole became a tunnel that extended about ten feet back into the rock. It was smooth except for the troll claw marks.

When we reached the end of the tunnel, Birgitte said, "This is where the Ruseol dwelled for the last four millennia. I can still feel its presence, but also its fear." She dipped her hand into her pouch and extracted more sparkling powder. She instructed me to turn in a tight circle as she blew the powder onto all the exposed rock surfaces. She whispered some words in Elvish and a brief blue light flashed. "I hope that helps," she said. "We can leave now, Pippin."

When we emerged from the hole, it seemed that all of the collected fey and dwarves had been holding their breath, because they all sighed and smiled. Aliiana laid her hands on the granite again and nodded. "Yes, that's better."

We left the chamber and retraced our steps through the twisting tunnels. We gathered again in the main dining chamber to discuss the next part of our mission.

"How can you possibly find the Ruseol?" Gornak asked. He looked miserable, and rested his head on his crossed arms.

"Pippin can track the troll's scent," Aliiana said.

"And after visiting the site where the Gem dwelled, I can feel a very slight presence of it, somewhere to the east," said Birgitte.

"We should get our bags packed and ready to set out again," said Nelathen. He turned to Gornak. "May we replenish our supplies from your stocks?"

Gornak absently waved his hand, sending his goblet splashing. "Of course." Then he slammed down the goblet. "But I'm coming with you. It's my fault that the Gem was stolen. I'll be responsible for the end of magic if we don't find it."

"Do we anticipate danger?" I asked, my ears drooping.

Aliiana patted my head. "I'm afraid so, Pippin. Only a very powerful dark wizard could have stolen the Gem. And that wizard will not want to give it up."

We set out a few hours later with our packs stuffed full. Gornak had outfitted himself for the journey with a large battleaxe and a pointed steel helmet. He wouldn't be able to pass for a human like Nelathen could.

I took the lead, with Aliiana on my back and my snout to the ground. The troll scent was strong and bitter, prickling my sensitive nose. The troll's trail headed generally eastward, winding through the valleys. The next few hours passed unremarkably. The trail wove around pines and spruces, and birds flitted above. The early spring air was chilly, but the sun was clear and warm.

After a while I had become so accustomed to the troll's scent that I was able to pick out other scents on the trail—a human and another creature. I mentioned it to Aliiana.

"A human?" she asked. "But they don't have magic. I can't imagine how a human could even know about the Gem, let alone control a troll."

That evening as we set up camp, we talked more about the theft.

"I think we should prepare ourselves for the worst," said Nelathen. "A dark wizard of unknown race who has placed a human, an elf, a dwarf, and a troll under duress."

"Who could do that?" I asked.

Nelathen shook his head. "I don't know." He twirled a fallen leaf around in his fingers as he considered. "I'll attempt to contact the Queen to find if any elves have been reported missing." With that, he walked a little way from the camp and sat down cross-legged in front of a large pine tree. With my exceptional Corgi ears, I could hear his heart and breathing rates slow to nearly undetectable. He stayed in that meditation for nearly an hour, then slowly rose and returned to the fire.

We all looked up at him expectedly. He shook his head and sat down. "No elves have gone missing recently, but the Queen reminded me of something that happened nearly ten years ago." He paused, and continued in a soft voice. "A wise elf named Baern disappeared mysteriously. He was a powerful wizard, and the Queen's council could not determine how he had been abducted. He was missing for months, and when he reappeared he had lost his memory—and his magic. Without the magic of the elves, he was no longer immortal. He rapidly aged and died."

"How could he lose his magic?" asked Aliiana.

Nelathen shrugged. "No elf has ever lost his magic in the twenty thousand years we've been in this land."

The next few days passed in the same manner. We continued to follow the trail as it wound east through the forest and gradually lost elevation. On the fourth day out, we ran into the first booby trap.

Chapter 5

The mysterious Angarath must have known or suspected that he would be followed.

That morning, I was in the lead as usual, following the troll's scent when another smell tickled my nose. *Mmmm... rabbit!*

Rabbits are fun to chase. I slowed a bit to sniff the rabbit's trail. Aliiana was deep in discussion with Birgitte, and didn't notice my distraction.

Sniff sniff sniff... I crouched low and padded as quietly as I could. I spotted the rabbit. He was crouched in the grass, a ray of sunlight illuminating his ears. I was such a clever hunter that he hadn't seen me yet. *Sneak sneak sneak.* I tip-toed to within a couple feet of the rabbit and pounced.

Mid-pounce, I froze. It was as if time stopped. There I was, balanced precariously on my rear paws, with my front paws in the air. In my peripheral vision I could barely see that Aliiana was half-fallen from my saddle, hanging in midair. I couldn't move a single muscle, and gravity didn't pull me down as it should have.

The rabbit was frozen, too.

"Stop! Stay back," Nelathen ordered the others.

Gornak grunted. "Stasis field."

I heard Birgitte's wings buzzing near, and then away to my left. She buzzed back from the right a moment later. "It's about thirty feet in diameter."

"How do we disarm it?" asked Gornak.

"The spell is usually anchored on an object," said Nelathen. "If we can destroy the object, that might nullify the spell."

I was aware of the others prowling around the perimeter of the stasis field. "There," growled Barrol. "That reddish rock looks like it's directly in the center of the field."

"I'll try to shoot it," said Nelathen. He circled around to the side, readied his longbow and notched a red-feathered arrow. He drew back and released. The arrow flew a few feet and stopped dead, floating immobile in the air.

"Oops," he said.

"All right, I'll give it a try," said Birgitte. She dipped her hand into her tiny bag and pulled out a bit of the sparkling powder. She worked the powder between her hands, forming a rod shape. Pointing the rod at the anchor rock, she spoke a few words in Elvish.

A brilliant green light blasted forward from her hands. It penetrated the stasis field. Hooray! We would soon be free.

But the green beam immediately slowed. We all watched as it decelerated to an agonizingly slow pace, eventually coming to a full stop just a few feet from the anchor rock.

Barrol snarled. I would have growled if I could have moved my vocal cords.

Nelathen sat down hard on the ground, elbows on his knees and face in his hands. "I'm so sorry, Aliiana, Pippin. I'm not sure what to do."

"What if..." Gornak tugged on his braided beard. "What would happen if the stone were to move?"

"The field would move as well," said Birgitte. "But how do you propose to move the rock when we can't enter the field?"

"There might be a way with dwarven magic." Gornak approached the edge of the stasis field. He lay down on his belly and pawed in the dirt and rocks of the ground. After a few minutes, he said, "I've reached a large slab of limestone. I just hope it extends far enough."

Gornak took out a small metallic tool from his belt. It gleamed as he carefully scratched a symbol into the limestone. Then he chanted in the harsh Dwarvish language and a blue aura developed around the symbol. When the glow reached a brilliant turquoise he shouted, *"Barnâkh,"* and pointed with the tool. The blue light flowed from the symbol across the ground, under the stasis field, and popped the anchor rock up, throwing it several feet to the side.

The stasis field followed its anchor, and Aliiana, the rabbit and I were released to fall to the ground. I hit the ground, rolled away from the stasis field, stood up, and shook myself from nose to tail. I was so happy that I ran over to Gornak and gave him a lick on his hand.

"Pippin," Aliiana said sternly, "you need to be more careful."

I drooped my big ears. "Yes, Mistress. I promise I won't chase any more rabbits."

The following night, we set up camp like usual. Nelathen and Gornak stretched out the elven tarp and Aliiana built a fire. Birgitte was really too small to do anything physical, but she used her magic to set a protective ward against intruders. Barrol bounded off into the woods to hunt.

Gornak called out after him, "Bring me back a hare, too!" Then he mumbled to himself, "I'm getting tired of this elven bread. Doesn't properly fill up a dwarf."

Barrol returned shortly with blood on his muzzle, holding two hares in his mouth. He dropped them in front of Gornak and purred. It was just like the purr of a regular kitty, but loud and deep, rumbling like a diesel engine.

"Excellent," Gornak said. "We'll have a feast tonight." He set about skinning and dressing the hares and stuck them on green branches to roast over the fire.

The fey wrinkled their vegetarian noses in disgust, but I drooled. I'm a carnivore, after all, and I was tired of elven bread, too.

Gornak and I ate our fill of roasted hare. Barrol had already eaten several fresh hares, and declined the roasted meat. He said cooking meat ruined it, but I thought it was delicious. With my tummy pleasantly full, I curled up near the fire and fell asleep.

We had been setting a rotation of watches every night, just to be safe. I usually took the last watch of the night. Sometime in the middle of the night, when Aliiana was on watch, I felt her little hand on my head.

"Shhh… Wake up, Pippin," she whispered. "I think there's someone out there." She quietly woke the others as well.

Birgitte fluttered above the remains of the fire. "The wards haven't detected anyone."

I heard a rustle in the woods behind me. I spun around and growled low in my throat. Even with my night vision, I couldn't see anyone.

Barrol suddenly snarled and leapt forward. At the same moment, Nelathen yelled behind me and I heard the clang of his sword. I heard more rustling all around us and realized that we were surrounded.

I finally saw one of the intruders. It was insectile, about six feet long, and had dozens of legs and four black eyes as big as grapefruits.

A giant centipede.

My hackles rose and my ears pinned back. I'm used to bugs being tiny. A bug as big as a sofa was not my idea of fun.

The ghastly beast made dry rustling and clicking sounds as it scurried forward on its many feet. I wasn't sure what to do. I was vaguely aware of my friends engaged in battle with other centipedes. Nelathen and Gornak swiped with their sword and axe, and Aliiana and Birgitte cast magic spells. Barrol tore into another centipede with his claws and fangs.

The gigantic bug continued to clitter-clatter toward me, and I backed up slowly, still growling. I suddenly remembered seeing border collies herding sheep, running around them, ducking low, and even jumping onto a sheep's back. I decided to try that with the centipede.

I held my body low to the ground and zipped around to the left of the beast. His four eyes saw me move, but he couldn't turn fast enough. I ran around behind him, nipped at the heels of his rearmost set of legs, and jumped up onto his back.

He turned his head around to glare at me. It was at this point that I noticed that below the four black eyes were two enormous red pincers, each dripping a viscous, medicinal-smelling liquid. I barked at him, but that only seemed to make him more determined to impale me.

The pincers snapped right in front of me. I jerked my paw out of the way just in time. Then he lashed his head around the other way, nearly snipping off my ears. I was about to become bug food.

I only had one chance. I barked at him again. His head whipped around, pincers glistening. Right before the pincers made contact with my shoulder, I jumped down to the ground. Instead of piercing tender Corgi flesh, his pincers pierced through his own tough hide.

The bug made a shrill sound and collapsed, twitching. I had won!

I quickly surveyed the scene around me. There were seven centipedes dead on the ground, and Nelathen and Gornak were finishing off the last two.

Aliiana sat down, panting from exhaustion. I went to her and licked her face. "I'm glad you're okay, Pippin," she said.

"Are you all right, Mistress?" I asked.

She nodded. "Just tired. Casting that many spells takes as much energy from my body as running all day would."

I looked at Birgitte. She must have been drained as well, because she wasn't even flying. She sat on a log, her green wings hanging limp.

We had all survived, but Barrol had suffered a cut on his leg from one of the centipedes. When Birgitte recovered her breath, she looked at the cut. "I don't think any venom got in the wound," she said. "You're lucky, Barrol. It should heal fine if you keep it clean."

We all sat around the dying embers of the fire, breathing hard. "Birgitte," Aliiana asked, "why didn't your wards detect the centipedes?"

"I think it's because I set the wards against sentient beings. The centipedes weren't sentient creatures. I think they were mindless slaves, doing the bidding of Angarath."

"Then he must know where we are," Gornak said.

"Aye," said Nelathen. "He must be using some sort of scrying spell. We need to be especially careful to avoid more attacks."

The rest of that night was free of incident, although none of us slept well from nervousness. The next morning, my friends tried to figure out a way to prevent Angarath from scrying us.

I learned that 'scrying' meant to cast a spell on a liquid surface to see the image of a person or scene far away. Angarath only needed to concentrate on the locations he had passed to see if anyone was following him.

"Perhaps a cloud spell to obscure his vision?" asked Aliiana.

Nelathen frowned. "But if a cloud is following us around, that will make us more conspicuous to humans."

"Invisibility?" asked Birgitte.

"Yes, that would work, of course. But maintaining an invisibility spell for that long would be extremely tiring."

"Can you scry him back?" I asked. If we could see where he was—and who he was—it would make our job easier.

"Good thought, Pippin," said Aliiana, "but unfortunately without knowing what he looks like or where he is, we can't target him. He can scry us because he knows where to look."

"Do any of you know an anti-scrying spell?" asked Gornak. The others all shook their heads.

"I think the best we'll be able to do is a diffusion spell," said Aliiana. "It would blur the image of us. He'll still know where we are, but he won't be able to see the details of what we're doing."

Gornak grunted his assent. "Well, let's see if we can combine our efforts, to make it as strong as possible."

Aliiana, Nelathen, Gornak and Birgitte all stood in a circle (well, Birgitte wasn't standing but was hovering like a hummingbird) and began to chant—three in Elvish and one in Dwarvish. A light yellow glow spun like a whirlwind in the middle of the circle. As it spun faster, it turned peach and then pink, colored like a sunset. They all released the spell simultaneously, and the spinning glow *poofed* and expanded to cover all of us.

It didn't feel any different, but when I looked at the landscape outside the spell I perceived a very slight fuzziness. Aliiana assured me that Angarath's view in his scrying bowl would be a big fuzzy nothingness.

The trail had been leading nearly straight east since we left the park. We had gradually come down from the Rocky Mountains into the foothills. We were about two-thirds of the way across the state of Montana, according to Nelathen's map, when the putrid troll-scent trail suddenly turned south.

My sniffer led us to the edge of a large lake surrounded by dried brown grasses and cattails. The ice was breaking up with the warming spring temperatures, and there were sharp ridges where sheets of ice had smashed into each other over the course of the winter. In some areas, the ice was white or pale blue, but in other areas it looked black and rotten.

Gornak peered at a black patch. "That doesn't look safe to cross."

"You dwarves are just afraid of water," said Barrol, curling his big furry lips into a smile.

"Be nice," Nelathen chided Barrol. He pulled out his map again and pointed to a spot at the edge of a large blue mark. "This is Fort Peck Lake. If we went all the way around it to the west, it would add a good sixty miles to our route. I don't like to think of Angarath getting that much farther ahead of us." He looked at Aliiana. "What do you think?"

"I agree," she said. "I think we should chance it on the ice and go across the lake."

"All right," said Gornak. "But I suggest we take some precautions before we cross." He surveyed us and our equipment. "I think Barrol and I probably weigh the most, so we should each walk alone. I would suggest that Aliiana walks apart from Pippin. And I would also suggest we tie a rope around our waists in case the ice breaks underneath one of us."

Everyone nodded in agreement. Nelathen took out a fifty-foot length of elven rope from his pack—very lightweight and very strong. He looped it around our waists at intervals of ten feet: the dwarf at one end, then himself, me, Aliiana, and then Barrol at the other end. Birgitte could fly over the lake safely.

"Ready?" Gornak asked. We all nodded, and carefully stepped out onto the treacherous ice. It wasn't really any different than walking on the snow and ice-crusted rocks of the mountains, except that I knew there was a freezing watery death just a few inches below my paws.

We were a couple hundred yards out onto the lake when a malevolent thundercloud boiled up right above us.

My first thought was, *Bad luck to be caught in a storm.* But before I could comment to my friends, a tornado's funnel dipped down from the thundercloud, and I realized the storm was yet another trap by Angarath.

The cloud spun rapidly, turning from grey to purple to black, faster and faster, towering up into the sky. It touched down on the ice in front of us and shattered it. Shards of ice rose up to join the whirlwind.

Birgitte was thrown down by the wind, and smashed onto the ice near me. She was so tiny, I was afraid she might have been killed. I hurried over to her and gently picked her up in my mouth.

"Hurry!" Nelathen's shout barely reached me over the howling wind. We were already running as fast as we could, scarcely making headway against the wind and flying ice chips.

We aimed toward the far shore, trying to bypass the hole that the funnel cloud had punched through the ice.

Crack!

A huge chunk of ice broke away, spinning off into the choppy water. Gornak had been standing on that patch of ice, and when it spun away he was dumped into the water.

He sank like a rock.

The elven rope must have still been attached to Gornak, because Nelathen was pulled over onto his back by the rope around his waist. He was dragged along the slick ice toward the hole. I knew that I would be next to be pulled down into the icy water.

Chapter 6

Aliiana's voice sounded in my mind. *Hang on, Pippin. I'll try to get help. I just hope there's a water fairy in this lake.*

I tried to dig my claws in to stop my slide across the ice, but the surface was slushy and I couldn't get a grip. I was pulled several feet towards the hole.

Squinting through the swirling storm, I saw Nelathen wrap the elven rope around the hilt of his sword and ram the sword into the ice to stop our slide. Then he pulled the rope up hand-over-hand from the freezing depths.

To my other side, I saw Aliiana sit down in the slush, oblivious to the whirling tornado, and place her bare hands on the ice. She closed her eyes and must have been chanting—I couldn't hear anything over the roar of the wind but her lips were moving.

Tied as I was to the rope between Nelathen and Aliiana, I couldn't move toward either one without disturbing the other, so I stood still, continuing to hold Birgitte in my mouth. She wasn't moving at all against my tongue or lips and I feared the worst.

At last! rejoiced Aliiana's voice in my mind. She stood up and looked toward Nelathen, who was still pulling on the rope.

Aliiana, Barrol and I hurried across the slush to the hole. As we watched, Gornak's head popped above the surface. Nelathen grabbed the dwarf around the shoulders and heaved him up onto the ice. Gornak was unconscious, his lips blue and his beard soaked.

Nelathen pounded on the dwarf's chest, then bent his head to listen for a heart beat. He shook his head, and pounded again.

A new face popped up from the water. It was a water fairy. She was similar in size and build to Aliiana, but had pale bluish skin and tangled wet hair. She looked at Aliiana and said, "He has inhaled too much water and may not live."

The water fairy climbed out of the hole and knelt next to Gornak. She placed her tiny blue hands on his chest, closed her eyes, and chanted in Elvish. A blue glow sparkled around her hands and his chest.

Gornak's eyes flew open. Nelathen quickly helped him sit up, and Gornak coughed, blinked and looked around. His eyes settled on the water fairy, and he asked in a hoarse voice, "Did you save me?"

She nodded but didn't speak.

"What is your name?" he asked.

The water fairy seemed to be very shy. She glanced back at the hole, then said, "Lennali."

Gornak bowed his head. "Thank you, Lennali. I owe you a debt—you and the entire fairy race."

Lennali smiled and dove back into the water.

The funnel cloud was losing its energy. Gornak was able to walk, although he had to stop to cough every few paces. We slowly made our way to the far shore.

We stepped off the ice onto solid land. By unspoken agreement, we made our way up onto a little hill before stopping.

Nelathen knelt before me and I gently placed Birgitte on his outstretched hands. There were tears in his eyes as he put a fingertip against her chest.

"I can still feel her heart beat," he said. "She's probably in shock. And her injuries..."

One of Birgitte's pale green wings, delicate and beautiful as a butterfly's, was shredded, the papery tissue hanging in limp threads.

"I can stabilize her," said Nelathen, "but I can't heal her wounds." He looked at Aliiana and Gornak. Both shook their heads.

Holding his hand above her tiny, broken body, Nelathen whispered an Elvish spell. A yellow glow surrounded her and her breathing became stronger, but she remained unconscious.

"We must get her to a healer," said Aliiana.

Nelathen nodded. "The nearest elven community is quite a ways to the south, in the Bighorn Mountains of Wyoming." He turned to Gornak. "Is there a closer dwarven community?"

Gornak shook his head.

"Then we must hurry to the Bighorn Mountains." Nelathen placed Birgitte in his knit snowboarder hat to keep her warm.

Gornak coughed again, deep racking wheezes that made his body shudder. When he was able to catch his breath, he spoke. "I know a spell for endurance, so we can avoid stopping to rest. But when we reach our destination, we will need to make up the sleep."

"Do it," said Aliiana.

Gornak nodded. He pulled out the metal tool I had seen when I was trapped in the stasis field. Now that I got a better look at it, I realized it was a miniature copy of his battleaxe. He knelt on the ground, brushed away a patch of snow, and carved a strange symbol into the rocky ground.

"A rune," Aliiana whispered to me. "The dwarves channel magic through symbols called runes, as I channel it through stone."

Gornak finished drawing the rune and muttered a few Dwarvish words. Suddenly, I felt as fast and strong as a greyhound. I could run all day and all night.

We made excellent time to the Bighorn Mountains—now that we weren't being delayed by Angarath's booby traps. Nelathen led us to a grove high in the mountains. As we approached, he whistled a complicated bird song. We heard an answering whistle high in the trees, and halted.

Nelathen removed his sword and bow and placed them on the ground. He nodded to the others, and Gornak laid down his axe and Aliiana her bow.

A wiry elf appeared from behind a tree. "Ahh, so it's you, Nelathen. I haven't seen you in seven decades."

Nelathen bowed low. "Darnel. It's good to see you. We're in desperate need of healing."

Darnel lifted an eyebrow. I suppose we all looked healthy to him. "Of course," he said. "Follow me."

Nelathen and the others picked up their weapons and we all followed Darnel. Unlike the dwelling of the Prince, which was tucked under pine trees, this was high in the air. A series of wooden platforms connected the trees fifty feet above the ground. Rooms were divided off with hanging green silks, and birds twittered in the trees.

We were led to a large platform, draped in light green gauzy fabric. In the chamber sat a beautiful elf with snow-white hair and flowing lavender gown. "Welcome," she said.

Nelathen bowed, and the rest of us followed suit. "Greetings, fair Princess."

A Princess? I bowed as low as I could on my short legs.

The Princess smiled. "Nelathen. My brother said you might be in the area. This must be Aliiana." She looked at me. "And you must be Pippin."

I barked and wagged my stubby tail. She laughed, like tinkling bells. Turning to Gornak, she asked, "And who is our dwarven cousin?"

"Gornak, ma'am," he answered, and bowed.

"But Darnel said you were in need of healing?"

"Aye," said Nelathen, pulling the red knit hat from under his cloak. He gently lifted Birgitte and approached the Princess. "She was injured in a storm and has been unconscious since."

The Princess gasped. "Poor thing..."

"Can you help her?" asked Aliiana.

The Princess held her hand above Birgitte's body for a moment. "She has broken ribs and brain injury. We can heal those, but..." She gestured to Birgitte's wing. Where the fragile tissue had been torn by the ice, the wing was now dry and brown, like a leaf dying in autumn. Several brittle pieces had already broken off. "We have no magic to regenerate limbs." She looked at each of us in turn. "She will never fly again."

The Princess turned away again and called to one of her attendants. "Please summon Zane." Turning back to our party, she added, "Zane is one of the strongest elven healers I have ever encountered. We will combine our healing spells."

A few minutes later, a young male elf entered the chamber and bowed to the Princess. She stood and placed Birgitte's broken body on the cushion of her chair. She and Zane linked their left hands and placed their right hands on Birgitte's body as they chanted in Elvish. It was a longer spell than most I had heard, lasting for nearly five minutes. As they chanted, wisps of white light flew into the chamber and congealed around Birgitte.

At last, the Princess and Zane released the spell and stood back. Birgitte blinked her eyes a few times and sat up. The dry brown bits of her damaged wing had all fallen off, leaving her with just a stub, only about a third of her wing.

Birgitte glanced around the chamber, stretched her arms and flapped her wings. She turned her head to inspect the damaged wing. "What happened?"

We told her about the ice tornado and our travel to the Bighorn Mountains. She listened calmly to the story, and didn't say anything about her disability. "Now you've lost the troll's trail," she said.

"Yes," said Aliiana. "But I think Angarath would have killed us with his booby traps if we had stayed on his trail any longer. We'll have to come up with another way to track the Gem."

Birgitte's eyes became distant. "I can still feel traces of the Gem from when Pippin and I entered the granite where it was hidden. It's faint, but I can tell it's east from here." She nodded. "We should set out immediately."

Gornak was overcome by another coughing spell. "We must stay here at least overnight to rest," he wheezed. "The endurance spell must be repaid."

"You are welcome to stay as long as you like," said the Princess. "I will have chambers and food prepared for you."

Birgitte nodded her acceptance and stood up on the cushion. She absently patted her waist. "My bag!" she said. "It's missing."

"It must have fallen off in the ice storm," I said.

Birgitte was considerably more upset about her missing bag than her damaged wing. "I can't do magic without *tlaelar* dust," she said. "I need to find a new supply." She turned to the Princess. "Are there any sprites in this elven community?"

The Princess shook her head. "I'm sorry. I don't know of any sprites in these mountains."

Birgitte wrung her hands and paced back and forth on the chair cushion. She muttered in such a high-pitched voice that I couldn't understand her.

In a few minutes, one of the Princess' attendants beckoned to us.

"Birgitte?" Nelathen asked the distraught sprite. "May I carry you?" She nodded but said nothing.

We followed the Princess' attendant up, down and around a series of platforms. She led us to a room high in an ash tree, draped in dark green silk on the outside and white on the inside. Smaller chambers had been divided off from the larger chamber, and were filled with large, soft pillows. In the main chamber a table was heaped with fruits and elven bread. Although the elves don't eat meat, they had arranged some dried meat for the cougar, the dwarf and me. We ate our fill and retired to the smaller chambers to sleep.

The next morning I woke up feeling especially well-rested and refreshed. I suspected there might have been a spell around the tree to ensure peaceful rest. We ate another meal and packed our bags with fresh supplies.

Aliiana hopped onto my saddle and looked around for Birgitte. "Are you ready?" she asked Birgitte.

Birgitte still sat at the breakfast table and her anxiety was plain. Her face was gaunt and her wings were limp. Her voice was high-pitched as she said, "I can't continue the mission."

Chapter 7

Birgitte was normally calm and rational, so the change in her demeanor was alarming. "I can't go with you," she said, tears streaming down her green face. "I need to locate my kin to obtain more *tlaelar* dust."

"We can come with you," said Aliiana. "Where is the nearest sprite community?"

"I searched telepathically. The nearest sprites are southwest of here, near the hot springs."

"We would be happy to take you to your kin," I said. She seemed to calm a bit, but I noticed her tiny hand kept straying to her belt, where the bag should have hung.

"Birgitte," said Aliiana. "Would you like to ride on Pippin with me?"

Birgitte looked at her ruined wing and nodded. "Yes, thank you."

Aliiana modified the saddle with some borrowed elven fabric, and when she was done Birgitte was able to sit comfortably and safely in front of Aliiana on my back.

We took our leave of the Princess and her court, and set out to the southwest. Nelathen and Barrol were in the lead this time. Barrol ranged out far ahead of our party, and came back periodically with reports of the terrain ahead of us.

Within a few hours we came to the hot springs. We carefully made our way through an alien landscape of terraced pools and gurgling springs. There were pools of every color—greens, yellows, rust, orange—and they emitted steam that smelled like rotten eggs. Gray and brown mud puddles popped and spluttered.

It seemed like a harsh place for the tiny, delicate sprites to live. I took the lead so Birgitte could navigate us through the hot springs. After we circled a large pool that spattered globs of pale tan mud, she told me to stop.

"The rest of you cannot go past here," she said. "My kin are not very welcoming of strangers. If I could still fly, I would go alone, but with my injury I will require Pippin's assistance."

Aliiana dismounted and retrieved her equipment. She looked around, and pointed to a small rocky hill with a dense stand of shrubby trees. "We'll wait for you in the trees," she said.

I barked to my mistress and turned back to the path.

"You'll need to be careful, Pippin," said Birgitte. "Sprites aren't always very nice to outsiders. I think you'll be safe because of your fey blood. No other creature would be allowed to approach."

I wondered what the sprites would do to me if they decided they didn't like me.

We reached an area where the minerals from the hot springs had built up a large rounded hill. The mound looked like a birthday cake, with waves and swirls of white and yellow, but the frosting was rock. The smooth stone curved down in layers, leaving a few gaps between the formations.

Birgitte steered me to one of the gaps. "In here," she said. "You might need to duck your head."

The gap was barely big enough for me to squeeze through. We found ourselves in a cave, with faintly glowing creamy rock walls and stalactites hanging from the ceiling. A brighter yellow light spilled from a cavern ahead.

"Slowly now, Pippin," whispered Birgitte. I tiptoed forward as quietly as I could.

Suddenly, the floor beneath my feet glowed blue. I hastily tried to pull up a paw but my feet were stuck fast to the floor, like I'd stepped in a puddle of superglue. It wasn't painful, but I was effectively immobilized.

A sprite appeared in front of us, a glowing blue rod in his hands pointed at us. "Who are you?" he demanded.

"I am Birgitte, of the Faille Clan. This is Pippin, my escort."

"And why did you bring an animal in here?" he asked, pointing the blue rod directly at my head.

Birgitte slowly slid off my saddle, hands in the air. She turned slightly so that her damaged wing was visible. "I require an escort because of my injuries."

The sprite squinted at her wing, then nodded. "He may enter. But if he tries anything, I'll blast him." The blue glow disappeared and my paws were free. "Why are you here, Birgitte of the Faille Clan?" he asked.

58

"I'm on a mission of importance to all fey. I've lost my *tlaelar* dust and need more."

The sprite frowned. "Come," he instructed, and flew to an opening halfway up the cavern wall.

Birgitte climbed up on my back, and I jumped to the hole, barely making it. It was a smaller chamber, lit by the same creamy glow. There were six or eight sprites here, fluttering around and talking. I was surprised that they weren't all green like Birgitte. There were also blue, yellow, and purple sprites, all with lighter colored hair and wings and darker clothing.

A lavender sprite fluttered toward us with a glowing yellow orb held menacingly in her hand. "A sprite from another clan has never dared ask for our *tlaelar* dust," she said. "Explain yourself."

Birgitte introduced herself again, and explained our mission to find the Gem, as well as the circumstances of her injury and the loss of her bag in the ice tornado.

The lavender sprite fluttered back and huddled in conversation with a yellow sprite. I couldn't hear what they said, but the yellow sprite kept looking at us and gesturing threateningly with another blue rod.

The other sprites spread out in a circle around us. Suddenly the blue glow popped up on the floor again, and my paws were trapped. Then it crept up my legs to my chest and tummy, and up the saddle to Aliiana's legs. I regretted wondering what the sprites would do to me if they didn't like me.

Chapter 8

"Excuse me," I said. "I apologize for entering your cave without permission. But our quest is important to all fey, including the sprites. Birgitte wouldn't ask for your dust if it wasn't important."

Finally, the yellow sprite spread his arms and retreated. The lavender sprite gestured to the others. She waved a hand and the sticky blue glow disappeared. "Very well," she said. "We will allow you to harvest some *tlaelar*."

The first sprite approached us again and smiled. "Sorry for my rudeness earlier," he said. "I'm Frenel of the Dolan Clan. I'll show you to the plants."

"Plants?" I asked.

Birgitte patted my head. "*Tlaelar* dust is actually the pollen of a rare plant that is grown by the sprites. It's how we channel the Gem's magic, and we're very protective of the plants."

Frenel led us to a larger cavern. Bright yellow light shone from the cavern, and as we entered, I saw that the light was actually radiating from the flowers. The plants looked a bit like lilies, with green spiky leaves and golden petals.

A number of sprites buzzed around the flowers. Some carried small feathery wands, which they brushed on one flower and then another. "Those sprites are pollinating the flowers," Birgitte explained. She pointed to other sprites who filled small bags with the sparkling *tlaelar* dust. "And those sprites are harvesting the pollen."

"You may take as much as you need," said Frenel.

Birgitte took up one of the small pollen bags and stood up on my back to reach the flowers. A moment later, she said, "We're finished." She turned back to Frenel. "The Faille Clan is in debt to the Dolan Clan." They bowed respectfully to one another. Frenel led us back to the entrance and I squeezed out of the cave to rejoin our friends.

We resumed our eastward trek. We left the mountains and found ourselves travelling across wide grasslands. The wind stirred grasses taller than me— taller even than Barrol, and sage grouse bustled around us. We startled a herd of pronghorn antelopes, and they took off faster than I could hope to run. We headed east, then south, then east again as Birgitte's sense of the Gem shifted.

At some point we crossed into South Dakota. We had to bypass south to avoid the Black Hills and Mount Rushmore. Even though it was only spring, the human tourists were already out in droves in their minivans and SUVs.

One afternoon I caught a small brown blur in my peripheral vision. I turned and it was gone. A minute later the brown blur jumped in front of me and yelled, "Boo!"

It was a small weasel, brown and white. He stood up on his rear legs and gazed at me and my riders.

"Hello," said Aliiana cautiously.

"Bet you didn't expect to see me," the weasel said, and took off again. A moment later he was back, emerging from under a sage brush. "My mistress hoped you would come."

I was more than a little confused. Apart from my Corgwyn kin, the only animal I had met who could speak the human language was Barrol. "Who are you?" I asked.

"I'm Bak," he answered. "I'm a black-footed ferret." He stood up on his hind legs again and waved his black front paws. "See?" He had a long body and tail, and also had black markings around his eyes.

"And what are you doing here?" I asked. The ferret was jumping around and didn't seem to hear me so I asked again, "Why are you here?"

"My mistress sent me to watch for you."

"Who is your mistress?" Aliiana asked.

"Sandra. Of the Oglala Sioux." The ferret dashed around the sage brush again. "She felt evil pass by recently, and hoped that good would follow. She sent me to fetch you."

I was becoming suspicious of this hyperactive weasel. "To fetch us?"

"Yep," he said cheerfully. "Follow me!"

Nelathen and Gornak had joined us. They exchanged glances and shrugged. Nelathen turned to Aliiana. "Should we go with him?"

"I think so," said Aliiana. "If his mistress is a human, she must be a powerful wise woman to have a familiar. She may be able to help us locate the Gem."

We followed the ferret a mile or two to the south to a small house surrounded by cedars. He led us around behind the house, where a dark-haired human woman sat at a picnic table covered with books.

I was nervous about our group meeting her. The fey and dwarves have always tried hard to hide their existence from humans. I could pretend to be a dog, but the others were pretty conspicuous.

She looked up, smiled, and rose from the bench. She didn't seem surprised to see such a bizarre group wander into her backyard. "Welcome," she said, coming around the table. "I'm Sandra Two Crow." She gestured to the ferret, who had scurried up onto the table. "And you've met Bak, of course."

Aliiana stepped forward and introduced us all. "Pardon me for asking," she said, "but how do you know of the fey?"

Sandra smiled. "Most people don't. But in every culture there is wisdom which has been passed down for generations." She turned back to the table and hurriedly stacked the books on one end. "Please, sit down."

We all sat around the picnic table. Sandra poured glasses of water for everyone, and set out bowls of water for the cougar and me. "You're wondering why I sent Bak to find you," she said. "Last week, I felt a terrible evil nearby. I sensed non-human beings, and also sensed that a powerful force was being transported against its will."

Aliiana nodded. "Yes, an evil act has been committed."

Sandra gestured to the stacked books. "Those journals contain stories that have been passed down in my family. They tell of the other races on this planet, and of magic, and of good and evil. They also tell of the Ruseol Gem. Is that the powerful force I sensed?"

"Yes," Aliiana said. "The Ruseol Gem was stolen and we are attempting to recover it."

"Who stole it?" Sandra asked.

"We only know the name, Angarath, but we don't know who or what Angarath is," said Nelathen. "Does the name mean anything to you?" Sandra shook her head, and Nelathen continued. "We know the thief is a powerful dark wizard, who may have dwarven and elven wizards under his command. He also had a troll with him."

"Ahh…" Sandra nodded. "That explains the non-humans I sensed, and the great evil. And do you know why he stole it?"

"He left a message," said Aliiana. "It said, 'The power will be mine.' We assume he's trying to absorb the Gem's power for his own uses."

Sandra pulled a map from the stack of books and unfolded it on the table. She pulled a pencil from behind her ear and sketched in a path. "This is where I felt the Gem pass. They came from the west, swung down to the south, and then into the Badlands." She circled an area on the map. "I felt it in this area for several days, but now my sense of it has dimmed. I don't understand why." She looked up. "Can any of you sense it?"

Birgitte nodded. "I can sense its direction, which is east, but not its distance."

Sandra looked at her wristwatch. "My kids will be home soon, and it's best that they don't see all of you. They're not yet old enough to learn of your races. I'm afraid I can't come with you to help locate the Gem, but I can send Bak with you. He knows the Badlands very well."

Bak jumped around in excitement. "Cool!" he chirped. He seemed to have picked up a lot of human phrases. "This is going to be awesome."

Nelathen bowed to Sandra, and Aliiana shook her hand. "Thank you, Sandra Two Crow, for your help," said Aliiana. I barked my thanks as well.

We set off again, following the bouncing weasel as he scurried around sage and prickly pear cactus, zipping back and forth across our path.

"Can you get us to the area that Sandra circled on the map?" I asked. "If we can get close, I might be able to pick up the troll's scent again."

"Sure can, dude," he answered. He led us for several miles into the remote areas of Badlands National Park. Erosion had cut hills and mesas into the ground, revealing sedimentary rock layers in various colors—yellows, grays, reds, and even greens. Some of the mesas were topped with patches of grass and waving yellow wildflowers.

I nearly forgot what I was supposed to be doing when I saw the first bison. My Corgwyn kin have herded sheep and cattle with the humans for generations. The bison was like an overgrown fuzzy cow, and I was entranced. Aliiana had to tap me on the top of my head to remind me of our task.

I shook myself and trotted to catch up with Bak. Suddenly, I caught the unmistakable odor of troll—the fetid opossum scent I had tracked in Montana.

I barked to get my friends' attention. "The troll! I've got his trail."

"Excellent, Pippin," said Aliiana. She and Birgitte were still on my saddle as I took the lead with my nose to the ground.

Bak was excited about the adventure. "What's a troll?" he asked. Without waiting for a response, he continued, "Are they easy to fight? Do you think they like ferrets?"

Aliiana sighed and turned to the weasel. "Bak, we're going into a very dangerous situation. It will probably be best if you stay back, out of danger. And stay away from the troll—it would eat you as a little snack."

The ferret wrinkled up his tiny snout. "I'm tougher than I look," he said, and ran off in front of us. He pouted for the next few miles. He ran ahead of us, although he stopped every minute to make sure we were still following.

The troll scent grew stronger as we wound around the banded plateaus and rock outcroppings, deeper into the heart of the Badlands. Despite the spring tourism season, we didn't encounter any humans.

"We're getting close," I said. "The smell is getting strong."

As we walked, everyone fell into silence, anticipating the confrontation with Angarath. Barrol ranged out twenty feet in front of me, his hackles raised. Gornak drew his axe, and Nelathen strung his bow and checked his sword in its scabbard. From the shifting movements of my riders, I could tell that Aliiana and Birgitte were preparing magic spells. Even Bak ran close to us and was quiet.

"Magic," growled Barrol. "There's a ward here, I can feel it."

There was nothing visible to mark the first ward, but as we crossed a patch of reddish rock, I felt a slight coolness vibrating against my skin. It was like walking through a waterfall—the chilly sensation started on my nose and traveled down my spine as I walked forward. The emerald pendant around my neck felt cold.

"Humph," grunted Gornak. "It's a safe bet that Angarath knows we're here now."

The troll scent was so strong it made me sneeze. The trail wound into a narrow chasm that was shaded by pinnacles and spires above, and dead-ended at a blunt rock face. "It's here," I said quietly.

Everyone stared at the rock.

"It's booby-trapped," said Nelathen.

"Well, then we know for sure we're in the right place," said Gornak.

Birgitte leaned forward over my ears. "I sense dwarven and elven spells, and dark magic, too. It's definitely Angarath's work."

Gornak pulled out the miniature axe. "I'll try to cancel the dwarven ward, then you can work on the elven ward." He slowly approached the mesa and scratched a small rune in the rock. He said a word in Dwarvish, and a larger rune suddenly glowed white on the rock face. "Hmm," he muttered to himself. He looked back at the small rune he had carved, and added a few more lines and circles.

Aliiana whispered to me. "He can't erase Angarath's rune without risking the spell backfiring, so he has to modify it to a different symbol."

I realized my heart was pounding. The glowing white lines and circles of the large rune rearranged themselves, shifting around to form a new pattern. At last, Gornak stepped back and coughed a few times. "I still don't have all my energy back from drowning." He wheezed a few more times, and added, "But I've disarmed the first ward. It won't hurt us when we pass it."

Nelathen paced back and forth in front of the rock face. I couldn't see anything, but he seemed to be scrutinizing something. "No," he said suddenly. "No, it can't be. Never!"

"What's wrong?" Aliiana asked, hopping off my back to approach Nelathen.

Nelathen dropped to his knees and buried his face in his hands. "No, no," he said. I realized there were tears in his eyes when he looked up at us. "This elven spell… It's an incredibly complicated warding. It has the same signature as a ward that was cast years ago when humans encroached on the elven community in the ancient forests of the Pacific Northwest. There were several *maelathier* trees—sentient trees that are thousands of years old—that had to be protected at all costs. And that ward was cast by Baern."

"Baern, the elven wizard who…" Aliiana began.

Nelathen nodded. "Yes. Baern, who was abducted and robbed of his magic."

Chapter 9

"But that's impossible," said Gornak. "No one could steal another's magic."

"We don't know what might be possible to a user of dark magic," said Birgitte. "There were ancient races on this planet that consorted with demons. There may be dark spells that are beyond our imagining."

Everyone was silent, sitting or standing, staring at the mesa. How could we hope to defeat a dark wizard who had stolen the powers of a great elf?

"If Angarath was able to steal Baern's magic, might he also have stolen a dwarven wizard's power?" Aliiana asked.

"We can only guess," said Birgitte. "Do you know of any incidents, Gornak?"

Gornak shook his head. "Those of us who guarded the Gem weren't in close contact with the rest of the dwarves on this continent, except for sending status reports to the King."

Aliiana turned back to Nelathen. "Can you disarm Baern's warding?"

He shook his head. "I'll need help." He looked around, making eye contact with each of us. "Even with help, it may not be possible." He stood up, took a deep breath, and turned to face the rock wall.

He held his arms straight out to the sides and chanted in Elvish. Faint streamers of greenish-yellow light spun off the ends of his fingers, weaving toward the rock. The ribbons of light twisted around as if they were tying and untying knots. Aliiana, seeing what spell he was attempting, stood next to Nelathen, and soon strands of light from her hands joined his.

The strands twisted and turned, but kept bouncing back from the rock. Birgitte, still on my back, said, "Pippin, I need to get close to them." I trotted up behind Aliiana and Nelathen. Birgitte stood up on my shoulders and threw *tlaelar* dust on them while singing in Elvish. With Birgitte's strength, the green-yellow ribbons of light grew brighter and pushed harder against the rock.

I wished that I had magic to contribute, but Corgwyn can't cast spells. We do have a spark of fey magic in our being, though, so I pushed my cold wet nose against the back of Nelathen's leg and willed my strength into him. I felt a tingle from the Prince's emerald pendant, ringing through the silver necklace to my skin.

Suddenly, a red streamer of light burst from the rock face. The red ribbon twisted around the green-yellow one, like two snakes fighting each other. The red light slashed from side to side, and Nelathen and Aliiana's lights dimmed. Birgitte threw some more sparkling *tlaelar* dust on them, and their lights grew brighter and stronger.

The red and green light snakes continued to writhe, back and forth, closer and farther from the rock. Finally the red ribbon dimmed and Nelathen's light approached the rock.

In a last burst, the red light broke away from the rock and hurtled through the air, straight at Nelathen. It smacked him hard on the chest, knocking him back off his feet. I was still standing behind him, and he flew over my head and crashed on to the ground behind me.

I scrambled over to Nelathen and poked my nose against his neck. "I feel a pulse," I said.

Birgitte jumped onto his chest and lightly ran up to his face. She pulled open one of his eyelids and peered into his pupil. "That wasn't just elven magic," she said. "There was dark magic incorporated into the elven spell, and it was the dark magic that hit him."

"Will he be okay?" I asked.

By this point, the others had joined us, forming a circle around Nelathen's body. Birgitte looked up. "He's in a coma. I can't detect even a tiny piece of his consciousness. But his body is alive."

"We need to find a healer," Barrol growled.

"No," objected Aliiana. "We need to remember our mission. The wards are broken now, and we won't have much time to get into the mesa to find the Gem before Angarath attacks us."

"Aliiana is right," said Birgitte. "We'll have to leave him here and find a healer after we retrieve the Gem."

"I won't leave him," said Barrol.

"We'll need your help," I said to Barrol. "Remember, there's a troll in there."

Barrol snarled, showing his huge white fangs. He looked from me to Nelathen, then suddenly spun around. "Bak!" he growled.

"I'm right here," said the little ferret.

"I'm going into the cave with the others," said Barrol. "You stay here and guard my master's body." He leaned down and opened his jaws wide. "If anything happens to him, I'll eat you."

Bak seemed pleased to have a job. He hopped onto Nelathen's chest and stood up on his hind legs. He saluted the cougar with a front paw and bowed. "I swear I will protect him with my life," he said solemnly.

Gornak hefted his axe and strode toward the mesa. I trotted behind him, with the fairy and sprite on my back, and Barrol followed me. Gornak tipped the axe head toward the rock face and it slipped through. The rock looked solid and impenetrable, but it was a harmless illusion spell. We all passed through the illusion and found ourselves in a tunnel, dimly lit by a few battery-powered camping lanterns. The stench of troll was overpowering, and the air bristled with magic.

"Strange," whispered Birgitte. "The Gem should be straight ahead of us, but I still feel it to the east."

We slipped quietly down the tunnel. Angarath hadn't detected us yet. After about thirty yards, the tunnel widened out into a chamber. It appeared to be some sort of magical laboratory. There were racks of potions—various glowing fluids and gels in glass containers and silver dishes. Along one wall stood a large copper device with many twisting tubes and funnels. Silver mist seeped out of a large black cauldron, and a purplish haze clung to the rough-hewn rock ceiling.

Gornak had just stepped into the laboratory when an enormous, smelly, furry beast leapt out from the side, snarling at us. The troll swiped a huge paw at Gornak, who barely ducked out of the way. The troll's claws glistened as they swooshed over the dwarf's head and hit the cave wall, knocking off chunks of rock.

I was petrified with fear. The troll stood twenty feet tall, with a head the size of a small car, and had twelve-inch-long yellow teeth that dripped rancid, gooey saliva. The troll took another swipe at Gornak, which he tried to meet with his battleaxe. The axe blade bounced harmlessly off the troll's hide.

Barrol jumped over me and darted in toward the back of the troll's knee, trying to bite at him.

"Pippin, move!" Aliiana's voice broke my fear. I scurried forward, zigzagging to evade the troll. Aliiana spoke in Elvish and I knew she was casting a spell. A bolt of white light blasted through the air above my ears and hit the troll's arm. His fur sizzled a bit where the bolt had hit, but he didn't seem to notice.

"Try to get closer, Pippin," said Birgitte. I knew that if she had been able to fly, she would have been fluttering high above the troll, but I had to be her wings. I wove around the troll's legs, running as fast as my short legs would take me. Birgitte threw her *tlaelar* dust at the troll's hairy leg, and where the dust touched the troll's fur it congealed into a dark green gel. The gel spread along his leg, hardening as it went. He seemed to feel no pain, but the hard green crust on his leg limited his movement somewhat.

With the troll's movement hindered, Gornak was able to slash upward with his axe. He made contact with the troll's hip, opening up a foot-long wound. The troll finally noticed this injury and howled with pain or fury, putrid spittle flying from his mouth and dark brownish-red blood spraying from the wound.

The troll spun around, slamming a huge paw into Gornak's side, sending the dwarf crashing into the copper tubing.

I continued to dash around the troll's feet. Remembering my encounter with the giant centipede, I nipped at the troll's heel, but only got his thick fur, which left a nasty taste in my mouth.

Aliiana hurled more magic bolts at the troll. Most just sizzled in his fur, but a few reached his hide and did some damage. Barrol landed a few more bites. The troll seemed to be weakening, but was still swiping at us with his dangerous claws.

The troll swung at me again, coming from the side. I dodged but wasn't fast enough and Aliiana was knocked off my back. She landed hard on the stone floor and didn't move. I wasn't sure if she was hurt or just stunned, but didn't have time to find out. I stood over her to protect her with my body.

"I need a distraction, Pippin," Birgitte said to me, slipping off my back. She ran on tiny feet around behind the troll. I couldn't leave Aliiana, so I did the only thing I could think of to distract a ferocious troll— I barked.

Chapter 10

I yapped as high-pitched and loudly as I could. The troll bent down and snarled, his face close enough to mine that I could have counted every one of his teeth. His tongue was dark purple with waving fronds of flesh on the top. A long glob of saliva dripped onto my head. I knew I was about to be eaten when an orange light flashed all around us.

The troll stood up, squealed, and tumbled over onto his back, falling in slow-motion, knocking over potions and glassware.

I was panting and my heart was pounding. It was a few moments before I could move. I stepped to the side and looked down at Aliiana. She blinked and smiled, slowly rising to her feet.

"Are you all right, Mistress?" I asked.

She nodded. "He just knocked the wind out of me." She looked around at the others. "Go check on Gornak."

I hurried over to where Gornak lay in a pile of copper tubing. His eyes were open, but he wasn't trying to move. "Are you all right?" I asked.

He moaned. "My side hurts where the troll hit me."

I barked, and Birgitte hurried over. She gently laid her hands on his side, feeling for internal injuries. "It's going to bruise badly but I think you'll be okay," she said. She sprinkled some of her *tlaelar* dust on him and said a quick spell.

"Thank you," he said, standing up gingerly.

Aliiana had recovered from the fight and was inspecting the magic laboratory.

"Acids, absorption potions, diamond-tipped burrs," Aliiana said, looking at items on a workbench.

"And over here are transmutation and dissolution potions," said Gornak.

Birgitte peered into the cauldron. "This potion is radiating dark magic. Don't get too close."

"But where's the Gem?" I asked.

"And where's Angarath?" asked Barrol.

I heard a faint clatter in a far corner of the room and ran over to investigate. There was a small wooden door set into the rock wall. I pushed at it with my nose but it wouldn't budge. I can't turn doorknobs with my paws, so I barked to the others.

Gornak hurried over. "What have you found?"

"I heard a sound behind that door."

Gornak tried the doorknob but it was locked. He shoved at the door with his shoulder, then shrugged and hefted his axe. With one swing of the axe, the wooden door shattered and broke away from its hinges.

An arrow flew out through the remains of the door and clanked off Gornak's steel helmet.

"Get back!" he shouted, ducking around to the side of the doorway. I jumped around to the other side.

Gornak swung at the door again, bringing down the rest of the wood fragments. It was completely dark beyond the doorway.

Another arrow hurtled out but passed over Gornak's head. "Come out," he shouted at whoever hid in the dark. The only reply was another arrow.

The others had joined us, standing to either side of the open doorway. "We need some light," Gornak said quietly.

Aliiana stepped back a few paces to get the right angle and tossed a glowing orb of white light through the doorway. The orb hovered, illuminating a small room furnished with a bed and desk. A figure crouched behind the desk.

"Come out, Angarath!" Gornak shouted again. "We have you surrounded and we've killed your troll."

A faint voice said, "He wasn't my troll."

"Where is the Gem?" Aliiana asked.

"You can't have it."

Aliiana pursed her lips and put her hands on her hips angrily, even though Angarath couldn't see her. "We won't let you destroy the Gem."

Another arrow burst out of the little room, whizzing past my shoulder.

Time for a stunning spell, Aliiana's voice echoed in my mind. She climbed up onto my back. *I need you to be very fast, Pippin, and run through the doorway.*

Yes, Mistress.

"Now," she whispered. I rushed forward, keeping as low as I could. I even tucked my ears flat to make a smaller profile. As I burst through the doorway a blue light shot over my ears, smacking the figure behind the desk.

Aliiana hopped off my back and hurried to the figure, the glowing orb following her. The figure was short, with green skin and pointed ears.

"A goblin?" Aliiana said. I could hear the surprise in her voice.

The goblin was frozen stiff, except for his eyes, which darted back and forth between Aliiana and the doorway. Our friends now entered the small chamber.

"Can you release the spell on just his head so he can talk?" Gornak asked.

Aliiana waved a hand and the goblin's head lolled over.

"Where is the Gem?" Gornak asked.

There was fear in the goblin's eyes as he shouted, "I won't tell you anything!" Then he spat at Gornak. Barrol snarled and leaned close to the goblin, showing off his sharp fangs. "You can't have it," the goblin said in a quieter voice.

"We'll find it, one way or another," said Aliiana. "We have the ability to track it."

"What's it worth to you?"

Gornak frowned. "What do you mean?"

"Money," the goblin said. "How much will you pay me for it?"

Barrol snarled again. "I really don't think you're in a position to negotiate," he growled.

The goblin tried to ignore the cougar's threat. He turned to Aliiana. "If I tell you where the Gem is, I want one million human dollars."

She crossed her arms but didn't respond.

"You're pushing your luck," Gornak said. "How about, we won't kill you if you tell us where the Gem is."

He sighed in resignation. "It's not here. He took it."

"Who took it?" asked Gornak.

"Angarath."

"Then who are you?"

"Kiarng," the goblin replied.

"Then who's Angarath?"

"My boss." The goblin's eyes went wide. "He'll kill me if I tell."

"What if we protect you?"

"You can't," Kiarng said, his head hanging. "He's too powerful."

"We're powerful, too," said Aliiana.

Kiarng looked sadly at Aliiana. "Be that as it may, you're too late. He'll destroy the Gem before you can reach him."

"Why does he want to destroy the Gem?" Gornak asked.

Kiarng sighed. "Because he's mad. He wanted to use its power for himself—that's what all those potions and things in the laboratory were for. But no matter what he did, he couldn't open it to absorb the power. So he got mad and now he's going to destroy it instead."

Gornak casually spun his axe and leaned close to the goblin. "But that would mean the end of magic. And without the magic of the Gem, all the magical races would wither and die—goblins included."

"I don't want that. I just…" We waited as he gathered his thoughts. "I tried to take the Gem from him. I wanted to go to the elves, to get a ransom for it." He looked despondent. "I never meant for magic to end."

"Why did you stay here?"

The goblin shook his head. "He left me here with the troll. I couldn't leave the cave because of the wards on the entrance."

Aliiana spoke gently. "Where did he take the Gem?"

Kiarng shook his head again. "I'm not sure. He said he was going to find a ferment-lab."

"A ferment-lab? What's that?" Aliiana asked.

"I don't know," said the goblin. "Angarath just said it was a party-hat-acceleration machine."

"You mean Fermilab?" I asked. "The particle accelerator?" The others all stared at me. "My human family watched a show on *Discovery Channel* about it. It's near Chicago. Scientists study subatomic particles there."

"Yes, that's it," Kiarng said. "He said the party-hats go fast enough to destroy the Gem."

My friends looked at me blankly, so I hurriedly explained. "Everything in the universe—rocks, trees, you, me—is made of tiny cells. Cells are made of even tinier things called molecules and atoms. Even smaller, the atoms are made of subatomic particles. Scientists study them by making them zip around superfast."

Gornak grunted. "That doesn't matter right now," he said. "We need to get to Chicago." He straightened and replaced his axe in its scabbard.

"You'll never get there in time," said Kiarng. "He took an airplane."

"We can take a plane, too," said Gornak.

"No, we can't," I said. "You could barely pass for human if you got rid of your axe and helmet, but Aliiana and Birgitte certainly wouldn't. And animals aren't allowed on planes except in crates in the cargo compartment."

Barrol snarled. "I'm not going in a crate."

"And first we need to heal Nelathen," said Aliiana.

"What should we do with our new friend?" Gornak asked, gesturing to the goblin.

"Maybe we can find some elves on the way to turn him over to," said Birgitte.

Kiarng was still frozen stiff from the stunning spell. Gornak picked him up by his clothing and swung him over his shoulder like he was carrying a log. We picked our way over the broken laboratory equipment, past the troll's body, and out the tunnel.

As we exited the mesa, we saw Sandra Two Crow sitting cross-legged on the ground, cradling Nelathen's head in her lap. Her eyes were closed and she held her hands against the sides of his head.

Barrol bounded over. "What are you doing to my master?" he snarled.

She opened her eyes. "Healing him," she said calmly, unaffected by the cougar's fangs just inches from her face. "I don't know much about elven physiology, but my people have universal healing herbs which should help him regain consciousness." She waved at the ground around his body. There were several piles of fragrant plant material, smoking faintly. "Now, shush, I need to concentrate." She closed her eyes again.

Bak scurried out from behind Sandra. "Bear root, sage and sweetgrass," he said. "He'll be back to normal soon."

"How did Sandra get here?" I asked.

Bak bounced up and down with excitement. "I called to one of my black-footed ferret cousins, and sent him to Sandra. He can't speak the human language like I can, but he chirped so loudly that she knew there was something wrong. She followed him back here on Rusty, her horse." He pointed to a reddish-brown horse standing a little way down the chasm, calmly munching grain from a feedbag on its nose.

Gornak swung the stiff goblin down and leaned him against a rock pinnacle, then sat down and pulled some food from his pack. "We might as well get some rest while we wait."

We ate and drank, speaking quietly to avoid disturbing Sandra. The herbs gave off a sweet, strong odor, and their smoke swirled around Nelathen. After an hour or so, Sandra opened her eyes and took her hands away from his head. She smiled as his eyes opened.

Nelathen slowly sat up and looked around, taking in the presence of the petrified goblin and the Sioux wise woman. "I seem to have missed a bit," he said. We filled him in on the situation and the urgency of getting to Chicago.

"Tree portals," he said.

"Pardon me?" Gornak asked.

"That's the only way we can get to Chicago in time if he's got such a lead on us. We'll have to contact the dryads for permission to use the tree portals."

Aliiana spoke to Sandra. "You have helped us immensely, and we are in your debt. But I have another favor to ask of you." She gestured to the goblin. "Can we depend on you and your tribe to serve justice to this goblin?"

Kiarng hadn't spoken since we left the cave, but now he yelled. "No! You can't give me to that human."

I glared at him. "You're on federal land right now. Would you rather we turn you over to the United States government? I'm sure the human scientists would love to run some experiments on you." That shut him up.

Sandra smiled. "Yes, I'll take the goblin. He can help me muck out horse stalls for a few months until he feels adequately repentant for his actions."

"Thank you," said Aliiana. "The stunning spell will wear off in a few more hours."

Sandra pulled a length of rope from her saddle bags and lashed the goblin to the back of the saddle. She gracefully mounted the horse. "Bak," she said. "Do you want to go with the others on their mission or stay with me?"

The ferret looked back and forth between Sandra and our party. Curiously, he addressed Barrol. "It's been a great adventure with you guys, but I have to stay with my mistress." He saluted the cougar again, jumped to Sandra's boot in the stirrup, and scrambled up her leg to sit in front of her.

Sandra waved to us and spurred the horse to a trot. They were quickly out of sight.

Chapter 11

"Where are we going to find dryads?" Gornak asked.

"The Black Hills forest should be large enough for several dryad territories," said Nelathen. "We'll have to backtrack a bit and sneak around the human tourists again."

For a while, Barrol walked next to me. "You fought bravely, little brother. I never imagined a Corgi could stand up to a troll." I wagged my stubby tail at the compliment.

"I suppose you and Nelathen probably have lots of adventures," I said, "but this is my first adventure."

Barrol laughed, a deep purring chuckle. "Fortunately, most of our adventures are pretty tame compared to this."

We reached the Black Hills that evening, and it was obvious why the humans called them that. The forest was dark bluish-black against the tans and light greens of the surrounding prairie.

We continued hiking late into the evening to find a remote area deep in the forest to set up camp. The pines and spruces towered above us, and red squirrels jumped among the branches. Granite outcroppings jutted up through the dried pine needles covering the ground.

"I'll talk to the trees to try to locate a dryad," said Nelathen. He grabbed his longbow and left the camp soundlessly. Barrol bounded off as usual to hunt rabbits, and Gornak honed the edge on his axe. I fell asleep soon after eating.

The next morning when I woke, Nelathen and the others were talking over a breakfast of dried fruit and nuts.

"What did you find out about the dryads?" Aliiana asked.

"From the trees," Nelathen said, "I got the impression that there are three dryad territories in the Black Hills forest. The nearest one is about two miles away."

"What do you mean by territories?" Gornak asked.

"Dryads are territorial creatures," Nelathen said. "A territory is usually several square miles, and they will fight viciously if their territory is threatened."

"Do you think they'll help us?"

"I hope so," he said. "They're a magical race, after all."

"And what exactly are the tree portals?" I asked.

"It's a magical link between two trees in different places. Usually they're very old trees with enormous trunks."

We finished up breakfast, broke camp, and set out following Nelathen. Every so often, he would stop, lay his hands on a towering pine and close his eyes. After a few moments he would start walking again, sometimes in a different direction. After about an hour, we reached a dense stand of ponderosa pines. In the center of the grove was an exceptionally tall pine with a trunk eight feet across.

Nelathen laid his hands on the giant tree. Nodding, he said, "This is it. Now to get the dryad's attention..." He looked at us. "Barrol, Gornak, Pippin, it might be best if you wait over there." He pointed to the edge of the grove. "Aliiana, Birgitte, you can help me try to convince the dryad to help."

The dwarf, the cougar and I retreated to the edge of the grove and sat down. Gornak grumbled under his breath about "ungrateful fey." I swiveled my big ears around so I could hear the others as they tried to contact the dryad.

Nelathen put one hand on the huge tree trunk and worked a spell with his other hand. A pale green ribbon of light swirled upward, twisting gracefully. He released the spell, and stepped back to watch the green mist wrap higher and higher. The trunk was perfectly straight and branchless for the bottom forty feet. When the green ribbon of light reached the first branches, it sent tiny ribbons to wreathe around each branch.

From my vantage point, I watched the green light twist all the way to the top of the tree, some two hundred feet up. Then I heard an unearthly wail, and saw a small brown figure scurry down the trunk.

As the figure approached the ground, I realized that it was a small female being, about the same size as Aliiana, with bark-like skin the same orange-brown as the pine's bark and hair the dark green of its needles. And she seemed to be quite angry.

She yelled at Nelathen in a high-pitched voice, gesturing wildly with her hands. I couldn't understand her speech, or even identify it. It sounded like the chatter of little woodland rodents.

Nelathen held his hand out in a calming gesture. "I apologize for disturbing you. Please understand our task is most urgent."

She chittered again, and suddenly red squirrels high in the branches of the surrounding trees threw pine cones down at us. The pine cones weren't particularly dangerous, but they left nasty bruises when thrown from fifty feet up in the air.

Nelathen continued calmly. "You have every right to be angry at us for coming uninvited into your grove. I am Nelathen, son of Jillaen, who is daughter of Marolle. This is Aliiana of the earth fairies, daughter of Belian, who is daughter of Ronilean. And this is Birgitte of the sprites, daughter of Faera, who is daughter of Dantree."

The dryad calmed down a little with the formal introductions. She bowed her head, and said, "I am Pen, daughter of Ponl, who is daughter of Pefr." The others bowed their heads to her.

Aliiana spoke next. "I also apologize for disturbing your sacred grove. We are on a mission of great importance. The fate of all magical races, including yours, depends on us."

The dryad chittered again to the squirrels. I was afraid we were going to be battered by pine cones again, but instead the squirrels came down and gathered around the base of the dryad's tree. She still clung to the tree, her little hands and feet grasping the bark, but she came down to within a couple feet of the ground. "Explain," she said tersely.

With the squirrel audience behind her, Aliiana bowed again to the dryad and explained our mission.

"You believe this Angarath will destroy the Gem?" the dryad asked.

"Yes," said Aliiana, "and in so doing will end all good magic."

The dryad rocked back on her feet as she considered this. "The dryads must have magic to maintain the forests. I will help you."

Nelathen explained that we sought transport through the tree portals, and then waved the rest of us over and introduced us to the dryad. She peered at us suspiciously. "Never before have any beings traveled the tree portals but dryads and elves. But I will allow it."

We all bowed to her and murmured our thanks.

"Which destination portal do you wish?" she asked.

"Near Chicago, or anyplace in northern Illinois," I said. She looked at me blankly. We realized that she was completely unfamiliar with human cities and states. And since Corgwyn have difficulty with maps, I was at a loss of how to describe the terrain.

Fortunately, Aliiana was able to describe our destination. "East of here, the land becomes flat. There is a large river that twists and turns on itself, where many birds gather in the spring. Further east is another great river, this one fast and muddy. Then there are five lakes as big as seas. We want to be between the muddy river and the tip of the southwest lake."

That didn't make much sense to me, but apparently the dryad understood. She nodded. "Yes, there is a portal tree in that area. A white pine, very beautiful."

The dryad finally stepped from the tree trunk onto the forest floor. The squirrels ran up to her, chirping and swishing their fluffy tails. She shooed them away, and turned to us. "Come."

There was a depression in the ground next to the tree, encircled by two great roots. She stepped into the depression and disappeared. We followed one at a time. The depression was larger and deeper than it appeared from above, as all of us fit comfortably inside. Only Nelathen's head stuck out above ground level.

"You must each grasp one of the roots," the dryad instructed. Everyone who had hands grabbed a root. Barrol and I looked at each other, and then at the dryad. "You may use your mouths," she said. So I gently took a root into my mouth, tasting dirt and pine bark.

The dryad chittered in her own language, and my vision dimmed. I felt a peculiar twisting and squashing sensation. Then I realized that the root in my mouth had changed contour and flavor, and the air was suddenly twenty degrees warmer.

Nelathen said, "We're here. You can let go of the roots."

I spat dirt out of my mouth and looked around. We were in a similar depression, but this tree was smaller— only four feet across, and its bark was grey.

We heard chittering from high in the tree, and another dryad scurried down. This one was also female, but with grey skin and bluish-green hair. We all bowed to her, and Nelathen went through introductions again. This dryad was even less communicative than the other, and she scurried back up the tree, leaving us alone.

"Stay here," Nelathen said. "I'll try to figure out where we are." He adopted his human disguise and dashed off, leaving his sword and bow behind. He returned twenty minutes later and announced, "We're in White Pines State Park. It's about sixty miles to Fermilab. And we need to be *very* cautious—there are a lot more humans in this part of the country than we're used to." He looked at Barrol. "And no cougars, so they would probably shoot you on sight."

Chapter 12

As soon as we emerged from the forest, I realized how hard it was going to be to keep hidden from the humans. This was flat farmland, with scattered homes and barns. Many of the farm fields had been planted but the crops were mere seedlings, only poking up a few inches from the rich brown soil.

Roads crisscrossed the landscape, and we had to duck behind barns frequently to avoid being seen by humans. Within ten minutes, it was evident that we needed a new plan.

I remembered from Montana that an invisibility spell wasn't feasible. "I have an idea," I said. "The fey can become invisible at will, so it's the other three of us who are conspicuous. Could we do an illusion spell to make Gornak look more human? And maybe make Barrol look like, I don't know, a big dog? And I can be a regular dog."

Birgitte nodded. "Good idea, Pippin." She dipped her little hand into her pouch and drew out more sparkling dust. "I need to put this on your heads." Nelathen gently lifted her and held her over Gornak and Barrol. The powder glowed and poured down in liquidy sheets over their heads and bodies. The glow faded and the illusions were complete—Gornak looked like a short, stocky human in faded jeans and a sweatshirt, and Barrol looked like a huge St. Bernard.

Barrol looked down at himself. "This is embarrassing," he growled. "Swear you won't ever tell anyone about this."

Nelathen, Aliiana and Birgitte shimmered lavender and then became invisible, along with their equipment. Gornak's equipment was disguised by the illusion, but he still clanked as he walked. My saddle was still visible so Aliiana dug out a piece of black cloth to wrap around it. It would blend with my fur at a casual glance.

We walked along the roadsides, seemingly just a human trailed by his St. Bernard and Corgi. We made better progress this way. I had to tell Gornak to relax and wave at farmers as we passed—his rigid stance and insistence on staring straight ahead were still too conspicuous.

We made camp that night hidden behind a dairy barn, and rose early in the morning before the farmer discovered us.

As we got closer to Chicago, there were more and more humans walking and driving around. From the slight shimmers in the air, I could tell that Nelathen had to duck out of the way of human pedestrians a few times to avoid being run into.

The Fermilab campus was easy to find. I knew the particle accelerator itself was underground, and the land above remained wild, with wetlands, prairie, and a captive herd of bison. As we walked along the perimeter, a man with a chocolate Labrador retriever stopped us. The Lab sniffed me and Barrol, and growled when he caught the strange cougar scent.

"Curious hunting dogs you've got there," the man said.

Gornak was still uncomfortable with his human disguise. "Pardon me?" he asked.

The man gestured to us. "Well, a St. Bernard and a Corgi aren't common duck retrieving breeds. Aren't you here to use the dog training area?"

"Oh, yes, of course," Gornak stammered. "Yes, exactly, we're here for dog training."

"The dog training area is over towards the east side." The man waved at the prairie. "If you just follow the main road, you'll find it near the nature area."

"Yes, thank you," Gornak said, and we hurried along. We entered the compound from the west, passing under a three-legged black archway.

"Strange," the invisible Aliiana said. "If Angarath is here, he's probably making quite a mess. I would expect a high alert situation from the humans. But I don't see any police cars or fire engines."

"For that matter," said Nelathen, "there don't seem to be any humans around at all." Just beyond the black archway stood a small building that I guessed was an official guard station for checking IDs, but it was empty.

We cautiously walked along the central road. "That's the main administrative building," I said, gesturing with my snout at a building shaped like an upside-down Y. The parking lot was full of cars. A few yellow school buses idled at the edge of the parking lot, and their drivers sat unmoving.

"How are we going to find the Gem?" asked Gornak.

"The goblin said he was going to use the particle accelerator," I said. "We'll need to get into one of the buildings and down underground."

"What exactly does the accelerator do?"

"It's a huge ring with magnets to speed up the particles," I said, remembering the television show my humans had watched. "The scientists run protons and antiprotons around in opposite directions and slam them into each other to see what happens." Gornak still didn't understand. "My guess is that he'll put the Gem in the pathway of the collision to try to destroy it."

"You're pretty clever, little brother," said Barrol.

"Which building do we need?" Gornak asked.

"I'm not sure," I confessed. "The television show wasn't geared toward people trying to break into the facility."

As soon as we stepped onto the sidewalk on the opposite side of the parking lot, I knew we were making a horrible mistake. I wanted to get away from Fermilab as fast as I could—away from Illinois, away from the Gem, away from the fey. I turned tail and trotted back to the main road.

"Stop!" Aliiana yelled from my back. "Pippin! Slow down!"

I just kept running, picking up speed. I swerved towards a clump of shrubs near the road, running fast and ducking under a low branch to scrape Birgitte and

Aliiana off my back. I heard them both thump on the ground but didn't look back.

Running at a full gallop, I was almost to the guard station when Nelathen scooped me up, grabbing me around my chest. I tried to bite him but he was too quick.

"Pippin, stop," he said. "It's a compulsion spell. You need to relax and remember our mission."

I stopped squirming and looked around. Now that I knew about the spell, I could sense it. It was a simple bit of magic for Angarath, a compulsion spell to prevent unwanted company while he worked. Anyone who approached the lab would feel an overwhelming desire to leave.

"I'm okay now," I said. Nelathen put me down, and I hurried to the shrubs where Aliiana and Birgitte were picking leaves and twigs out of their hair. The fey were all visible now, my antics having broken their concentration. The illusion spell was broken also, destroying Gornak and Barrol's disguises.

"I'm sorry, Mistress," I said to Aliiana. "I feel awful for leaving you."

She patted my head. "It's okay, I know it was just the spell. But you'll need to be alert for other spells." She turned to the others. "Let's check out the main building first."

As I stepped up onto the sidewalk again, I told myself, *It's just a spell, it's just a spell.* I felt like running away again, but was able to mentally block it out. We cautiously approached the administrative building and peered through the glass door.

We discovered why we hadn't seen any people.

An ugly greenish-brown fog crept along the floor of the lobby, eddying and swirling like a stream. Through the fog, human bodies were visible sprawled on the floor. Some people slumped in chairs or against countertops. All were unconscious—or maybe dead.

"Let's go around to the other side," said Gornak. Behind the building was the ring, marked by a road and earthen berm. I knew that the accelerator was twenty-five feet below ground level. We could see quite a few industrial buildings and power stations around the four-mile circumference of the ring.

"How will we know which building Angarath entered?" Aliiana asked.

Barrol growled. "We could just follow the bodies."

We all turned to look where Barrol indicated. A human lay unconscious by the side of the ring road. It was an older man and he wasn't moving. Further along the road another body sprawled, this one a young woman with a yellow hard hat.

I started towards the man to check for a pulse. Aliiana spoke gently. "We must find the Gem as soon as we can, Pippin. We can care for the humans later."

I nodded, and we all hurried along the ring road. A quarter of the way around the circle we came to a short concrete building marked *Authorized Personnel Only*. Another body lay on the sidewalk in front of the building.

"In here," said Nelathen, trying the solid steel door. It was locked. I sniffed around, looking for another entrance.

"We don't have time to waste," Gornak muttered. He looked at the electronic keypad on the wall next to the door, then hefted his battleaxe and bashed it. The keypad shattered, a tangle of multicolored wires popped out, and there was a click as the door unlocked. Gornak chuckled as he hauled the steel door open.

I held my breath, expecting more of the toxic brown-green fog, but the air was clean. The door opened onto a cinderblock hallway with harsh fluorescent lights overhead.

"I sense the Gem ahead of us," said Birgitte. "I think we're getting close."

We hurried down the empty hallway to a red door that was marked *Tevatron*.

"That's it," I said, and pushed my nose against the door. We hurried down two flights of stairs to a control room. Dozens of monitors lined the walls, and computers hummed in the background.

A young woman sat in one of several swiveling office chairs, encased in a block of ice. Only her arms and head stuck out of the ice. Her black hair was matted and there was fear in her eyes. She glanced at us as we barged through the door, then returned her attention to a dark figure in the corner.

Chapter 13

I only had time to turn my head toward the dark figure before I felt a scorching heat growing under my skin. It was a terrible pain, and I felt like my fur would burst into flames. I howled and backed up.

Barrol snarled and leapt over me toward the dark figure. He crossed the room in two bounds, but Angarath casually waved a hand, sending an invisible force that knocked the cougar back to the opposite wall.

Within the span of a few heartbeats, the small control room flared with magic. Aliiana and Birgitte threw spell after spell but Angarath easily batted them away. Nelathen and Gornak circled around to either side, trying to get close.

"Hot, hot, hot," I growled. I still felt like my skin and fur were bristling with flames, but I knew I had to do something to help my friends. *Ice*, I thought. I ran to the young scientist imprisoned in the block of ice, jumped onto her lap, and pressed my body against the cool surface. I sank into the ice a few inches as my heat melted it. "Much better," I said. The woman was still trapped and looked terrified. I gave her a lick on her cheek to reassure her and jumped down.

Nelathen had drawn his long sword. The blade gleamed in the fluorescent light as he slashed the sword with his right hand and tossed glowing white magic missiles with his left.

Angarath stepped forward to meet Nelathen's attacks. He was dressed in black and red, with a billowing dark cape. He wore a necklace with an *A* picked out in rubies against an onyx background.

I looked closer at his face and blinked in surprise. "You're human," I said.

Angarath looked down at me with disdain. "Yeah, so?" he said. "Yeah, I'm a human. And you're a dog."

"I'm a Corgi."

"Whatever." He threw a spell at Gornak, hitting him in the chest. Gornak grunted and stumbled back, clutching his chest.

Nelathen shouted, "You destroyed Baern!" as he slashed with his sword, nicking Angarath's upper arm.

"Was that the elf?" Angarath taunted. "Or the dwarf? Or a human?" He chuckled. "I lose track, I've destroyed so many."

Birgitte had climbed up onto a desk and taken cover behind a computer monitor. She worked her *tlaelar* dust in her hands, forming rods of light to hurl at our enemy. The spells hit him, but didn't do much damage.

Angarath glanced sharply at the young scientist. She had been rolling the office chair toward the door. He yelled, "Stop!" and threw a red streak of magic at her.

She winced when it struck her face and wheeled the chair back to the computer console.

"Get the Tevatron online *now*," Angarath ordered her.

She nodded and tapped on the keyboard. "Yes, sir," she said. "The proton and antiproton streams are in the main injector now, sir."

I spared a moment to look over at Barrol. He was still sprawled on the floor where the force wall had hit him. He wasn't moving.

Angarath dodged a blow from Gornak's axe, striking back with a flaming whip of dark energy. "You think you can stop me?" he shouted.

"We will stop you," Gornak wheezed. It sounded like his lungs weren't yet back to normal after nearly drowning.

"You're a fool," said Angarath.

"Why do you want to end magic?" Nelathen asked, swinging his sword.

Angarath magically produced a black blade and swung it to meet Nelathen's sword. When the two struck, sparks of blue and red fell to the floor. "You elves just think you're so superior. I asked Baern to teach me elven magic and he refused," Angarath said.

"But what about all the other magical races?"

Angarath grunted. "That flea-infested dwarf wouldn't teach me magic, either. The world will be better off without all you freaks!"

"How did you steal their magic?" Nelathen huffed between sword swings.

"By being smart," Angarath said. "There are much more powerful beings on this planet than you pointy-eared tree-huggers."

"But you'll lose your magic, too."

"Wrong again, elf. The Gem is the source of *good* magic, but I happen to have arranged another source for my magic."

Gornak ducked to avoid the black blade. "An evil source."

Angarath shrugged. "Whatever works."

Gornak swung again and again with his battleaxe, but the deadly blade missed by a tiny fraction every time.

"You stupid dwarf," Angarath shouted. "You couldn't even hit the broad side of a barn with that toy. Let me show you what *real* power looks like." He waved his hands, forming a churning black cloud. The cloud twisted like it was alive and made growling noises. Angarath grinned, and hurled the cloud at Gornak.

Gornak screamed and toppled over onto his back. All his clanking armor couldn't protect him. The black cloud writhed and snapped as it burrowed between the plates of his armor and under his clothing. His screams grew higher and higher pitched as he thrashed around in agony.

Nelathen and Birgitte had momentarily stopped their attacks in shock at the horrific cloud eating Gornak, but they both gathered themselves and started again. Nelathen continued to swing with his sword, only occasionally touching Angarath, and Birgitte threw spells as fast as she could form her *tlaelar* dust. But they were both weakening. Nelathen's swings weren't as powerful, and it took longer for Birgitte to cast each spell.

Aliiana ducked behind an office chair and started chanting a complicated spell in Elvish. I didn't want Angarath to notice her casting, so I ran up to distract him. He didn't see me as I dashed close to bite his ankle.

"Aah!" he yelled. "That hurt, you stupid dog."

"I'm a Corgi!" I yelled as I zipped behind a computer which immediately exploded in sparks as one of Angarath's spells hit it. I took cover behind another office chair.

Angarath hadn't noticed Aliiana. A blue glow formed between her hands and she jumped out from behind the chair and threw it at Angarath. The blue light spattered against his chest, spreading out and sizzling as it burned his flesh.

The spell had injured him—but it had also infuriated him. "I'll kill you, fairy!" he screamed. He made another growling black cloud and hurled it at her.

The cloud snarled as it flew toward Aliiana. It knocked her over and surrounded her. Through our telepathic link, I felt her pain as the cloud chewed at her flesh. I could barely stand from the agony I felt from Aliiana. I howled in pain and frustration. I paced around the cloud, trying to see a way in to help her, but it completely encased her. I turned back to see Angarath swing his magical black sword at Nelathen, cutting deep into his upper arm.

"You elves are worthless," Angarath shouted at Nelathen. "How your race has survived this long is beyond me. But pretty soon you'll wither and die, and I'll be laughing over your rotting corpse." Angarath swung again, slicing across Nelathen's chest. Nelathen cried out in pain and fell backwards.

I looked around at my friends. Nelathen lay moaning on the tile floor, Barrol was slumped unconscious, Birgitte was panting with exhaustion, and Gornak and Aliiana were both surrounded by growling clouds.

Angarath had won.

Chapter 14

Angarath strode over to the young scientist. "Do it *now!*"

Her hands shook as she typed. "Yes, sir." A tear slid down her cheek, and she clicked a red button on the computer. A loud whirring sound grew around us, louder and louder until it sounded like an airplane flying low overhead. "Any second now, sir," the scientist said. Her computer monitor flared bright green, then went dark.

I whimpered. The Gem was destroyed. Aliiana would weaken and die without its magic, as would all the other fairies, elves, dwarves and sprites. I had failed my mistress.

Through my link with Aliiana, I felt her pain worsen every minute. Her skin burned as the cloud dissolved through like acid. It pierced all the way down to her bones, and then scraped out along the bones to her hands and feet. I desperately wanted to help her, but didn't know how to fight the cloud.

Evil. Aliiana's voice rang in my head.

Angarath was certainly evil—he was willing to destroy magic because of his jealousy. I needed something good to fight his evil. But what could I do? I was just a Corgi, without opposable thumbs or weapons or magic. All I had was my saddle, my collar, and the necklace from the Prince.

The necklace.

I remembered it tingling when I tried to help Nelathen disarm the wards in South Dakota. And the Prince was certainly good—he wanted to preserve the source of magic.

I lowered my head and pawed the necklace off. It landed on the tile floor and I looked at it closely. The emerald pendant was in the shape of a leaf, inlayed with tiny silver veins. I picked it up in my mouth and looked at Angarath. He wasn't paying attention to me, so I dashed behind him, shifting the necklace in my mouth. I chomped down hard on the back of his leg with the emerald on my tongue.

"Aah!" he shouted, louder this time.

I held on tight while Angarath kicked. I suddenly smelled the pines of the Prince's mountain home, and heard the clear voices of singing elves. And through my telepathic link with Aliiana, I felt her pain disappear, replaced by a sense of relief.

Angarath's shout turned to a scream, and he fell forward unconscious. I lost my grip on his leg as he thumped onto the tile floor. The black clouds around Aliiana and Gornak disappeared. I ran over to Aliiana. Her skin was red and pock-marked, but she was able to stand on wobbly legs. Gornak was in worse condition. His beard and clothing were torn, his skin was raw and bleeding, and he was moaning.

Barrol and Nelathen both hobbled over.

"He destroyed the Gem," I said sadly. Nelathen slumped down and buried his face in his hands. Barrol leapt forward and swung his open jaws toward Angarath's throat.

"No," Birgitte said, coming out from behind the computer monitor. "We shouldn't kill him; he should be brought to justice."

"But he deserves to die," Barrol growled.

"We cannot say who deserves to live or to die," Birgitte objected. "If we killed him, we would be no better than he."

"Birgitte is right," Aliiana said weakly. "But we must bind him, and keep him unconscious until he can be brought to trial."

"Bind him with the necklaces," I said. "Their good can defeat his evil."

Nelathen tied up Angarath with his strong elven rope, working with difficulty because of the deep cuts on his chest and arm. Aliiana gathered all our necklaces and looped them around Angarath's arms and legs, making sure the emeralds touched his skin.

"Wait," said Birgitte. "I still sense the Gem."

The others looked up. Aliiana whispered a simple spell and a glowing yellow ball appeared in her hand. "The Gem!" she said breathlessly. "I can still channel its magic."

Nelathen tested his magic, too, and cast a healing spell over Gornak.

Barrol approached the scientist and gently swiped at the ice block with his claws to free her. She stood up and brushed her hair back from her face. "Thank you," she said. "By the way, my name is Amy."

"Amy," said Aliiana, "where did he put the Gem?"

"In one of the detectors that monitor the collisions between the protons and antiprotons."

"How do we get there?"

"Quick, follow me."

Aliiana said, "Birgitte, Barrol, you two stay here and stand guard, and look after Gornak." The rest of us followed Amy down a short hallway and through a door marked *Restricted Access*. The door opened into the inside of a large white tube. Smaller metal tubes ran inside the big tube.

"It's this way," said Amy, jogging down the tunnel to the left. The detector was an enormous collection of machinery, with metal pieces as big as cars. "He made me put the Gem in here. I'll see what's left." She climbed under some metal parts and disappeared.

When she returned a few minutes later, her small body was bent under the weight of the Gem. It was just like the Prince had described—larger than me, oblong-shaped, and a brilliant reddish-purple color—and it seemed to be undamaged. It was faceted like a fancy diamond; there must have been thousands of facets, each sparkling in the overhead light.

Nelathen took it from her, staggering a step or two as he shifted its weight. We all hurried back to the control room, where the others waited with the unconscious Angarath. Gornak had recovered somewhat. He still looked terrible but was on his feet.

Birgitte rushed over and laid her tiny hands on the Gem. "It's unharmed."

Gornak gestured weakly at the room around us. "Even this enormous contraption couldn't destroy its good."

Aliiana and Birgitte wove a spell, creating a fuzzy halo of yellow light around Angarath's head. "That will keep him unconscious for a week," said Birgitte.

"Wait," Amy said. "You're going to attract a lot of attention if you carry that thing outdoors. It's sparkly enough down here. I've got a duffel bag in my car; it should fit." She started through the door and up the stairs to the main level. "Follow me."

Gornak swung Angarath's body up over his shoulder, grunting with the effort. We followed Amy up the stairs.

When we left the building, Amy saw the body we had passed on our way in. "Karl!" she shouted, running to the man and bending to feel his neck. "I feel a pulse," she said, "but he's unconscious."

"A stunning spell, most likely," said Aliiana. "It should wear off in a few hours."

Amy jogged to a silver compact car parked in front of the building and opened the trunk. She came back with a navy blue duffel bag and a white towel. "It's my gym bag, and you can wrap it in this towel for padding."

The Gem sparkled brilliantly in the sunlight, each facet reflecting a tiny rainbow in reds, purples, pinks and blues. It was so beautiful that I touched it with my wet nose as Nelathen wrapped it in the towel. I felt a hum through my nose, and it seemed that the Gem was happy.

Aliiana turned to Amy. "Thank you so much for your help. Don't go into the main administrative building—he released a poisonous potion or spell in there."

"Give us five minutes to get away," I said, "and then call 9-1-1." Amy nodded.

"And we'd appreciate it if you didn't tell anyone about us, or the Gem," Aliiana said.

Amy laughed. "Like anyone would believe me, anyway."

Nelathen hefted the duffel bag. Gornak still carried Angarath over his shoulder.

"We're even more noticeable now," I said.

Birgitte nodded, and wove a fresh illusion spell. She transformed Barrol back into a dog and Gornak into a human. The illusion included Angarath, too, disguising him as a cardboard box on Gornak's shoulder. The fey shimmered to invisibility, along with the duffel bag on Nelathen's back. I barked a final thanks to Amy, and turned to lead the others back to the main entrance.

When we were half a mile away, we heard the sirens.

Chapter 15

Several ambulances and police cars sped past us. I hoped the humans had survived Angarath's attack.

"We need to get out of the area fast," I said. The sirens were all behind us, but it was only a matter of time before the human police closed off the area. I knew from watching television news that if a lot of humans were injured, the roads would all be blocked and federal authorities would be called in.

"Where are we going?" Gornak asked.

"I think the safest place to take the Gem would be the Queen's land in Washington," said Aliiana.

"Aye," said Nelathen. "It's the most strongly warded area in the world."

I knew of the Queen of course—she had assigned me to Aliiana—but I had never met her, and didn't know where she lived. "Washington State?" I asked.

"Yes," said Aliiana. "In the ancient temperate rain forest of the Olympic peninsula. There's been an elven community there for over three millennia."

"How are we supposed to get from Illinois to Washington?" I asked.

"Not to mention while lugging the Gem and Angarath," said Gornak.

"We'll have to take a tree portal again," said Aliiana.

"I know a haste spell," said Gornak. "We'll be able to run very fast, but we'll be in terrible need of rest when we reach our destination."

"But if any humans see us running superfast," I said, "they might become suspicious."

"I think it's a risk we'll have to take," said Aliiana.

We ducked into an alley for privacy. Gornak put down Angarath's body—not very gently—and kneeled on the dirty pavement to scratch a rune. A pale blue light swirled up from the ground, surrounding us. He stood up blindingly fast and said, "Let's go."

We kept to alleys and back roads, and were quickly out of the populated area. The trek from the white pine portal to Fermilab had taken a day and a half, but our return trip only took three or four hours.

By the time we reached the forest, I was absolutely exhausted. I felt like I had been running without stop for days. It was evening, and we all slumped into the depression at the base of the portal tree. I don't think the dryad even noticed us as we all fell into a deep sleep.

We had all been too tired to post a guard, but fortunately we were undisturbed overnight. Barrol was the first awake and snarled, waking the rest of us. "We could have been attacked!" he growled at Gornak. "The Gem was in danger!"

Gornak frowned at the cougar. "I warned of the side effect of the spell."

"It's all right, Barrol," said Nelathen. "We need to summon the dryad now." He performed the same spell as he had in South Dakota, making green streamers of light wind around the trunk and branches of the pine.

The dryad screamed and chattered at us from fifty feet up the trunk. I got the picture that dryads didn't like company. Aliiana calmly spoke to her, introducing herself and Nelathen, but instead of cooperating, the dryad scurried higher up the tree.

Nelathen performed the spell two more times before the exasperated dryad finally came down to speak with us. Aliiana explained the situation to the dryad, and mentioned that Pen, daughter of Ponl, daughter of Pefr, had sent us through the portal previously. Perhaps Pen had a higher standing in dryad society, because the white pine dryad suddenly acted friendlier, although she still wouldn't give her name.

"Very well," she said. "Where do you need to go?"

"The Queen's land," said Aliiana.

The dryad nodded. "The golden *maelathier*—such a tragedy."

"Yes," said Nelathen, "a horrible tragedy."

The rest of us murmured agreement, although I had no idea what they were talking about. I turned to look at Aliiana questioningly. "Later," she whispered.

We took our places in the depression at the base of the pine. Nelathen still carried the Gem in Amy's duffel bag. Gornak propped up the unconscious Angarath and wrapped his limp arm around one root. I felt the squishing travel sensation again, and was suddenly aware of *life*.

I looked up at our destination tree. It was enormous and magnificent. The trunk was easily twenty feet across and covered with mosses and ferns. Everything around us was green, vibrant and alive. Mosses dripped from the branches and covered old logs on the ground like a carpet. I was entranced, having grown up in a desert.

The depression at the base of this tree was huge and lined with a soft bed of moss. "Let's rest a moment," said Nelathen, "and I'll explain some things." He squatted and lovingly brushed the moss with his hand. "I haven't been here in years..." He looked up. "As Aliiana mentioned, the elves have had a community here for over three thousand years. The Queen has lived here for two thousand, and the area has always been heavily warded for her safety. This kind of tree"—he gestured to the huge spruce above us—"is called the Sitka spruce by the humans. There are a few Sitka spruces with golden foliage, and they are sentient—the *maelathier*. One such tree was revered by the people of the human Haida tribe, and was a gentle and wise spirit. An ignorant, foolish human murdered that tree two decades ago. There are several other *maelathier* that the humans are unaware of, within the Queen's land. Because of the threat to them, Baern cast wards to protect this land—the most powerful wards ever cast."

"Are the wards still intact after Angarath stole Baern's magic?" Aliiana asked.

Nelathen nodded. "Yes, and they will persist until the end of the world." He stood up and looked around as if expecting someone. "The wards can only be passed by fey, and common animals." He looked at me and Barrol. "Because you two are familiars, you wouldn't be able to pass, and of course Gornak and Angarath can't pass. There's a gate through the wards which you'll have to use."

A petite female elf dropped soundlessly into the depression, a short sword in her hand. She spun around, flipping the tip of the sword up to Nelathen's throat.

Chapter 16

Everyone reacted immediately. Gornak swung his axe out, Barrol growled, and Aliiana and Birgitte started casting spells.

"Wait," Nelathen said. Curiously, he chuckled. "It's okay." He turned to the female elf and smiled at her. "I was hoping you'd be the one to find us," he said. He grabbed her in a hug and said to the rest of us, "This is Belara—my sister."

She smiled at all of us. "It's so nice to meet you all. Has my little brother been getting into trouble again?"

Gornak laughed. "No, ma'am, he's been getting us out of trouble."

"We need to see the Queen immediately," said Aliiana.

"Come then," Belara said. She raised an eyebrow as Gornak picked up the unconscious Angarath and swung him over his shoulder.

The gate was actually a tunnel that passed underneath another giant Sitka spruce, between its massive roots. We were instructed to walk through one at a time, although Gornak would have to drag Angarath behind him.

When it was my turn, I hesitantly walked forward, passing between roots larger than my body. I felt my fur prickling with magic power from my nose to my tail. A voice from nowhere asked my name and purpose.

"I'm Pippin the Corgi," I answered. "I'm accompanying my mistress and the Ruseol Gem." My brain felt like someone or something was picking though it, ruffling through my thoughts and memories to see if I spoke the truth.

"You may pass," the voice said.

I trotted out the other side as fast as I could, before the voice could change its mind.

The fey were already waiting, having simply walked around the tree. Aliiana and Birgitte climbed onto my saddle. "Welcome to the center of the fey civilization," said Aliiana.

Barrol emerged from the tree gate, looking anxious, and a few minutes later Gornak appeared, dragging Angarath by a foot.

"Let's go," said Belara. She and Nelathen walked in front, chatting happily in Elvish.

We hiked several miles deeper into the rainforest. The travel was slow, because we had to climb over fallen logs and duck under hanging curtains of moss.

At last we reached a small clearing. In the center stood two trees that I immediately knew must be *maelathier*. They resembled the ordinary Sitka spruces, but their needles were golden yellow instead of bluish-green. Magic waves rolled off the trees, and I felt a deep sense of peace.

A few elves in white and gold clothing approached us. "Welcome, travelers," said a female elf with dark braided hair. They fell into step around us as we followed Belara. Between the two golden trees stood a large building made of polished wood. It extended high into the air, and was decorated with carved filigree and leaf patterns inlayed with gold and green enamel.

As we got closer, I realized that although the structure was built very close to the *maelathier* trees, it didn't actually touch their trunks. We passed through an arched doorway into a circular room. A staircase spiraled up along the wall to the right, and a large round table stood in the middle of the room.

"This way," said Belara, leading us up the stairs to the next level. Many elves were gathered in this room. Sunlight streamed through arched windows, and an elaborately carved wood and gold throne stood in the center of the room.

I had never met my Queen, but recognized her immediately from her bearing. She was beautiful, with long golden hair and a light green robe. Her eyes were wise and her face ageless.

She rose gracefully from the throne, approached us, and addressed Aliiana. "I hope you have good news for us about the Ruseol?"

Aliiana smiled widely. "We do, Majesty." She nodded to Nelathen, who swung the duffel bag down from his shoulder, kneeled, and gently extracted the Gem from the towel wrappings.

The Gem pulsed slowly, a bright reddish light radiating from its center.

The Queen smiled. "Marvelous." She bent and placed an elegant hand on its surface. She closed her eyes and the rhythm of the light pulses quickened. Opening her eyes again, she said, "It is unharmed, and grateful for your rescue."

Gornak cleared his throat politely. "Here's the thief, Majesty," he said and unceremoniously dumped Angarath on the floor.

"A human?" asked the Queen. "However could a human have stolen the Ruseol?"

"Majesty," said Aliiana, "he appears to have studied dark magic, and with his dark knowledge he stole the magic abilities of the elf Baern and an unknown dwarf."

The Queen shook her head sadly. "We will arrange a trial, and justice will be done." She turned to another elf. "I must contact King Latrak." The other elf nodded, sprinted up the stairs, and returned with a golden bowl and pitcher, which he set on a small table.

The Queen poured a pale yellow liquid from the pitcher into the bowl, and waved her hands above the surface. The bowl rang with a metallic hum, and a dwarf's face appeared. The dwarf was older than Gornak, with grey hair and beard. He looked annoyed.

"What did you wake me up for?" he grumbled.

The Queen laughed lightly. "Latrak, I thought you might be interested to learn that the Ruseol has been recovered."

The dwarf sat up straight and leaned forward. "Thank goodness," he said. "May I see it?"

The Queen looked at Gornak. He picked up the Gem with gentle hands and held it in front of the bowl.

"Majesty, the Ruseol is safe," he said. The King said something in Dwarvish, and Gornak bowed.

The Queen stepped up to the bowl again. "Latrak, the dwarves have guarded the Ruseol for four thousand years. Now the guard returns to the elves."

The King nodded gravely. "Where will you keep it?"

The Queen turned to address our group and the collected elves. "Down through the millennia, the elves and dwarves have taken turns in guarding the Ruseol Gem. It has been hidden on every continent, and has been moved whenever threatened—sometimes as often as every decade. I think we will keep it here, with the *maelathier*. No place is safer."

"Excellent decision, Elspeth," said the King. "Now, I need to get back to my nap." He winked, and the image in the bowl went dark.

The Queen turned back to Gornak. "Would you please bring the thief forward," she said in a sad voice.

Gornak nodded and lifted Angarath from the floor, propping him up straight.

The Queen approached to stand close to Angarath. She reached out, not quite touching him, but holding her hands an inch away from his skin. "I sense the evil in his soul," she said. "The emeralds have suppressed the evil, but it still lurks underneath. We need to perform a ritual to pull the evil from him, and then we can proceed with a trial."

She sat back down in her throne and tapped her fingers against her lips. "Please fetch the entire Council," she said to Belara.

Within a few minutes, a dozen more elves had arrived in the throne room and it was getting a little crowded. Guessing an elf's age is difficult but the newly-arrived elves all had white or grey hair, and a few had subtle wrinkles—an aging sign that doesn't develop until an elf is at least a few thousand years old.

Everyone else in the throne room fell quiet. A few of the Council elves approached Angarath. Like the Queen, they didn't touch him, but moved their hands around him. Some muttered to themselves. "Evil," said one. "Terrible," said another.

The Queen and the Council elves formed a circle around Angarath, linking hands and chanting low. I only understand a bit of Elvish, but I didn't understand any of the words in the complicated spell. As they chanted, white streamers of light formed around Angarath, spinning and weaving into a net. The net was impossibly complicated, with hundreds of strands and knots. After about ten minutes, the elves all turned their faces upward and released the spell.

The net of white light snapped shut, encasing Angarath's body. The strands sank through his clothing and then through his skin. A sour-smelling puff of black burst away from his body and sank through the floor, never to be seen again.

The Queen thanked her Council and turned to us. "We have removed his connection to the dark magic. It was that dark magic which allowed him to perform the stolen elven and dwarven magics. Now that the evil is gone, he will be an ordinary human again." She waved a hand at Angarath to return him to consciousness.

Angarath's eyes snapped open. "What happened?" he demanded. Without waiting for a response, he chanted in a harsh language I didn't recognize. His pupils went wide and he shrieked. "What did you freaks do to me?"

The Queen approached him. "We have sliced away the evil from your soul. You are now unable to perform magic, and will be tried for the theft and attempted destruction of the Ruseol."

Angarath spat at her. "You elven garbage!"

"Do you admit to having stolen the Ruseol?" asked one of the other Council members.

Angarath sneered at the elf and struggled against the rope. "Of course I admit it," he said. "I'm proud of it! I'm the first human ever to outsmart you elves, and I'll do it again. You've got the Gem now, but it'll be mine again soon, and I'll finish what I started."

The Council elves all looked at each other, communicating telepathically. After a moment, the Queen spoke again. "You have been found guilty. You are sentenced to live the rest of your life here among the elves, cut off from evil and from magic."

Angarath howled.

Gornak stepped up behind Angarath and lifted him up over his shoulder. Angarath was still screaming, now carrying on about "crusty, smelly dwarves."

"Majesty," Gornak said to the Queen, "where would you like me to deposit the prisoner?"

"There's a room on one of the upper levels which should work nicely," she said. "It's made of wood, of course, but we can easily strengthen it with a spell. It will be absolutely secure. Plus, the window has a wide view of the forest, so our friend can contemplate the beauty and wonder of this world."

Gornak followed a pair of elves up the spiral staircase. He returned a few minutes later, chuckling. "He's screaming his head off up there about how unfair it all is. Personally, I think a long, quiet life surrounded by the serenity of the elves should do him good." Gornak handed out our silver and emerald necklaces, and returned the elven rope to Nelathen. "These won't be needed anymore."

"My friends," said the Queen, "let us adjourn for lunch, and then perhaps you would assist me in determining a new location for the Ruseol."

We all bowed, and followed her down the stairs to the main level, where the table was now heaped with breads and fruits. Even though the elves didn't serve any meat, the fruit was so fresh and delicious that I ate my fill.

While the others were finishing the meal and chatting, I wandered out of the building for a closer look at the *maelathier* trees. Their trunks were fifteen feet across, and bare of branches for the bottom thirty feet. The golden needles high above me glittered in the sunlight filtering down through the forest. I approached the left-hand tree very slowly.

I wasn't sure of the protocol or rituals required in making friends with a sentient tree. I assumed I shouldn't pee on it. I slowly approached the tree and gently pressed my wet nose against the rough bark. *Greetings*, I thought hard in my brain.

124

Greetings, it responded.

I was so shocked I jumped back involuntarily, then stepped forward and placed my nose on the tree again.

You have touched the Ruseol, the tree said.

Yes, we've recovered the Gem and it's happy, I said.

Where will it be kept for the next cycle?

Somewhere here in the Queen's land.

I know the perfect spot—a niche on my trunk a hundred feet up. The Gem and I will have long conversations over the next few millennia.

I barked and trotted back into the elven building, where the others were still lingering over their fruit.

"Majesty," I began, "pardon me for interrupting, but I was just speaking with one of the trees—"

"The *maelathier* trees?" she asked.

"Yes, Majesty, I apologize if that was inappropriate, but the tree said it has a hole where we can hide the Gem."

The Queen quirked a smile. "You must be a very special Corgi to have spoken with the trees."

I wasn't sure if she meant that as a compliment, or if she was chiding me for overstepping my bounds. "Yes, Majesty," I said quietly.

The Queen turned to the others. "Well," she said, rising from her chair, "shall we go see the hiding spot our clever *elranor* has discovered?"

We all followed her outside. She respectfully approached the tree, curtsied, and put her hand on the trunk. After a few minutes, she signaled to a couple of elves. "Rope, please."

The other elves pulled out lengths of elven rope. One bowed to the tree, put his hands on the trunk, and began to climb with the dexterity of a squirrel. He quickly climbed to a hundred feet, then threw down the rope end. The other elf, working from the ground level, tied a few knots and within minutes they had installed a pulley system.

"May we see the hole?" asked Aliiana.

"If the tree is agreeable," said the Queen.

Aliiana laid her hand on the trunk, and apparently the tree consented, because she was quickly hoisted up along the pulley system. Nelathen strapped the Gem in, and it too was lifted up into the air, now rapidly pulsing red and purple light flashes.

"Pippin," Nelathen said, "do you want to go up?"

Corgwyn aren't meant to climb trees or fly, but since I had made friends with the tree, I allowed myself to be strapped into the harness.

The ascent was frightening. I bumped into the trunk a few times, and felt queasy seeing my friends on the ground grow smaller and smaller. At last I reached the level of the niche and was extracted from the ropes.

This far up, the trunk was still at least ten feet across. There was an opening in the side of the trunk, as if a giant woodpecker had been at work. Through the opening was a cozy little chamber about three feet across, surrounded by the pale golden living wood of the tree.

Aliiana and the elf had already removed the Gem from its harness and had settled it at the back of the chamber. It glowed purple now, and I felt magic crinkle in the air between the Gem and the tree.

Aliiana said, "Farewell," to the tree and Gem, and the elf helped her back into the harness to return to the ground.

I hesitantly stepped forward, and stuck my nose against the Gem. Although it didn't communicate in words, its sense was joyous. Then I stuck my nose against the tree and thought, *Farewell.*

Farewell, little elranor, the tree responded. *Come back to visit.*

I barked with happiness, and allowed myself to be strapped in for another scary ride. After I was safe on the ground, the elves unhooked the ropes and pulley, and we went back into the Queen's home.

We spent a few relaxing days as guests of the elves—dancing and playing music, eating delicious fruits and breads, and exploring the forest around the *maelathier* trees, but then it was time to go home.

The Queen spoke with the dryad, who allowed us to use her tree portal. Gornak returned to Montana to meet his kin and travel with them to the dwarven homeland. Nelathen, Barrol and Birgitte went home to the elven community in the mountains, and Aliiana and I returned to the foothills south of the city.

When Aliiana and I reached her little home in the oaks and sage, she kissed the top of my head. "We did it, Pippin," she said. "You're the best Corgi steed a fairy ever had." I gave her a lick, and dashed off to the city.

When I reached my human home, I slipped under the gate into the backyard. The little girls were playing in the yard. They saw me, squealed, and ran over to hug me. "Mommy!" they called. "Mommy, Pippin's here! Pippin came home!"

Laura came out from the house laughing. "Pippin! We missed you." She picked me up, looked at my eyes and mouth, and felt my tummy and paws to make sure I was healthy. Then she noticed my emerald necklace. "What have you been doing, you clever little Corgi?" she asked.

I didn't tell.

About the Author

Laura Madsen is a veterinarian, mom, and writer. She has published many magazine articles for both children and adults. This is her first novel.

Laura lives in Utah with her husband, daughters, and Pippin the Corgi.

Find more about Laura's writing projects at:

laurambooks.blogspot.com

Follow Pippin the Corgi on Facebook at:

www.facebook.com/PippinTheCorgi